The singer paused on his way to the stage and took an audience member's hand, delicately pressing it to his lips. Everyone — or to be more precise, all the girls under the canopy — went wild.

The crowd jumped up and rushed forward as the singer took the stage. If only Alexis had sat closer to the stage. There was no way she could possibly catch his attention from all the way in the back. Who was this guy? How come she'd never heard of him — or how gorgeous he was?

border town

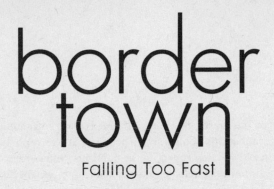

border town

Falling Too Fast

MALÍN ALEGRÍA

Point

Para mi papá

ISBN 978-0-545-40242-2

12 11 10 9 8 7 6 5 4 3 2 1   12 13 14 15 16 17/0

Printed in the U.S.A.   23
First printing, September 2012

De músico, poeta y loco, todos
tenemos un poco.

We have all been fools once in our lives.

chapter 1

"The funny thing about destiny," Alexis Garza said as she pulled open the storefront door, "is that sometimes it needs a little shove." Her friend Nikki Cantu giggled as she followed Alexis into the *botánica*. The narrow shop was dim and filled with magical wonders. On the crowded shelves there were crosses of various sizes, jars filled with herbs, and colored candles with labels like: "Money," "Luck," or "Stay Out of Jail."

"Look at this," Alexis said, picking up a box of soap. Nikki leaned over to see. There was a picture of a man and a woman surrounded by little pink hearts. Alexis read the Spanish label with a dramatic flair: "*Ven a mí.*"

"Ooooh." Nikki smiled. "I think that's a love soap. You wash with it and then guys can't resist you."

Alexis's eyes brightened. This was exactly what she needed to change her love life. Ever since her ex had smeared her reputation last year, no boy at Dos Rios High had asked her out. She felt cursed. Alexis had plenty of guy friends, but she wanted to go on dates and have someone to call her boyfriend.

"You girls looking for *amor*?" a low, decrepit voice called from the back of the room.

The girls jumped. Nikki crouched behind Alexis. The two girls had met in mariachi class last year and become instant best friends. Nikki was from an even smaller town than Dos Rios, right next to the Rio Grande River.

"Yes," Alexis said, louder than she meant to. She tried to stand up straight with her chest out like her grandma Trini showed her. Correct posture always made her look older than fifteen.

The old woman moved toward the girls. Dull gray linen hung loose around her shoulders and hips, making her look like an unkempt mummy. As the woman shuffled forward, Alexis felt a tingling sensation race up her spine.

"We want boyfriends," Alexis blurted out, turning red. She hadn't meant to be so bold. Their plan had just been to check out the store and see what kind of odd stuff it might have. But now, seeing the shop clerk, Alexis felt compelled to ask for help. Alexis had always been drawn to magic and mystery. As a child, she'd begged her grandmothers to tell her ghost stories before bed. Unlike her big sister, Fabi, Alexis loved to scare herself. Her favorite stories were of *La Lechuza*, a woman who sold her soul to the devil and could transform into a screech owl at night. Alexis shivered; maybe she was looking at the real *Lechuza.*

The woman grabbed a red candle and set it on the counter. She then reached for a bag of prepared herbs and a small feathery thing that looked like a stuffed bird. Alexis and Nikki inched closer for a better look.

"San Antonio is the saint of lost things. He'll help you find what your heart seeks. If he's stubborn, you can put him upside down in a dark oven until he brings you a boyfriend." She pointed a trembling finger at the bag of herbs. "This is a *baño de flores*, a flower bath created with the nectar of the hummingbird. The dead hummingbird is powerful. It brought me many men."

Alexis couldn't help but giggle. The woman recoiled, staring at Alexis with yellow eyes. Alexis felt her cheeks burn. "I'm sorry. I didn't mean —"

The woman raised her gnarled hand and grabbed Alexis's wrist. Alexis stiffened at the woman's iron grip. "You think I'm ugly," she snapped in a raspy smoker's voice.

Alexis swallowed hard, searching for something kind to say. "You have a very pretty smile," Alexis said finally. She jerked back when the woman opened her mouth to reveal rotting teeth.

"You lie," the woman hissed, giving Alexis the chills. "You see this" — she gestured at her rags — "and believe that this is how I've always been. I used to be the most beautiful woman in the Valley. But I was young and stupid. Don't you be young and stupid." The woman forced open Alexis's fist and traced the lines on her palm. "You will have two men come into your life." Alexis gasped, unable to hide her excitement. "One dark and the other light."

"Really?" Alexis gasped again. "What do they look like? Are they cute? Are they romantic? Will they fight over me?"

The woman ignored Alexis's questions. "Your cousin will lead you to one," she said. Alexis and Nikki raised their eyebrows at each other.

They bought two Saint Anthony candles and the bag of flower bath. When they got outside, Alexis howled with laughter.

"Could you believe her? Saying that she was once a beautiful lady." Alexis stopped to admire her own reflection in a store window.

Nikki glanced at the *botánica*. She was hugging herself despite the heat outside. "I think we should go. This place gives me the creeps."

"Oh, come on," Alexis teased. "Don't tell me you believe anything she said." Alexis rolled her eyes. "She's just playing a part."

"I don't know," Nikki said. "She looks pretty powerful to me. What if she puts a spell on us?"

Alexis burst out laughing. "Listen to yourself. She just wants us to buy things. And you never know, this stuff might actually work." Alexis shook the paper bag and grinned.

Although she swore the old lady was a fake, Alexis couldn't shake the feeling that her prediction, about a new guy coming into her life, was true.

So when she overheard her cousin Santiago talking about a drag race, her gut told her she had to be there with him. The palm reader did say that her cousin would lead her to one potential boyfriend. The only problem was that Santiago didn't want her following him around. This left her with no other option but to go undercover.

The night of the race, she tied her flat-ironed hair back into a ponytail and put on a pair of dark jeans and a black long-sleeved shirt. Her cousin would be pretty easy to follow. With his head of dark curls and his big black truck blasting Spanish music, he was hard to overlook.

As for sneaking out of the house, it would be easy. When your family owns a restaurant, there is always work to do. However, Alexis had certain privileges. She wasn't expected to work at the restaurant as much as her older sister, Fabi. Alexis's passion was music, and her family fully supported her dreams. Besides, with after-school mariachi rehearsals, violin practice, and homework, Alexis had a full plate. Earlier in the day, Alexis had told her mother an excuse about going to Nikki's house to practice for a school presentation. It sounded just plausible enough for her mother to wave her away without any questions.

Alexis was about to leave when she remembered the glow-in-the-dark face paint Fabi had used last year to scare a couple of bullies at the cemetery. Alexis giggled to herself as she rubbed the greenish-white paint on her cheeks. *Maybe I can scare Santi*, she thought, dabbing a couple of finishing touches onto her lips.

The sound of chirping *chicharras* in the night warned her that tomorrow would be another hot and humid day. Alexis stepped onto the wooden porch of her white bungalow-style home on the south side of Dos Rios. A smile crept onto her lips as she ran down the empty street toward her cousin's house. She was off on an adventure — maybe to find her destiny.

Her cousin's truck was parked in front of his place. Alexis thought about hiding in the bushes to scare him when he passed, but she didn't want to give him an excuse not to take her along. Instead, she decided to hide under a musty old serape in the bed of his truck. If she waited until he got to the races — or better yet until he was actually racing — then he definitely couldn't force her to go home.

Soon, Santiago climbed into his truck and peeled out onto the road. They drove for a while, out of town and into the barren landscape of the Rio Grande Valley. Alexis wished she could sit up and look for some distinguishing markers, anything that would tell her where she was. Her plan to scare Santiago and meet the guy of her dreams was starting to seem like a bad idea.

Suddenly, the truck came to an abrupt stop. Alexis could hear voices laughing and music playing from someone's car, but she didn't dare look out from under the blanket — not yet. Her cousin got out of his truck and greeted some passing people.

"You came," an excited male voice cried.

"Please. You practically begged me to come," Santiago replied in a confident tone. She recognized the sound of a slapping handshake. Was that one of the guys she was supposed to meet? she wondered. "Yo," her cousin asked, "so who else is here?"

The answer was cut short by the sound of a car honking behind them. "What the . . . ? Aw, don't tell me you invited those fools?" Santiago asked.

"Hey." Santiago's friend lowered his voice. "The Salinas brothers have a lot of cash. I don't know where they got it and I don't care. But they want to race *you* . . . only you."

"Who's that guy with them? I've never seen him around."

Alexis perked up. *A stranger?* She risked a peek in the side mirror — she didn't recognize the guy in the Salinas brothers' truck, but maybe he was her destiny? He was definitely her type: cute.

"So how 'bout it?" his friend asked, growing serious. Alexis jerked back down under her cover. She was dying for a better look at this stranger.

"Dude." Santiago cut him off. "I don't know. I promised my moms. I've got to keep a low profile. I'm already in enough trouble."

"Just one race. Look, I'll even sweeten the deal for you. I'll give you fifty bucks just to race. Win or lose."

The car behind them honked twice. A voice Alexis recognized as Brandon Salinas's called out. "So what's up? Is that punk in or out?"

Santiago sighed deeply. Then Alexis heard Santiago's friend say, "He's in."

Alexis's heart pounded frantically. She didn't know what to do. Should she come out from under the serape now, before the race? Drag races were off-limits. Her mother warned her and her older sister to stay clear of them if they didn't want a whack from their mom's floppy *chancla*. It was bad enough she was here at all, but to stay in the truck made her an actual *participant*.

Alexis thought about coming out of her hiding spot. Her cousin would be mad. But better he be upset now than later, when her body was thrown from the back of the truck. Alexis knew she would be a lot safer standing along the sidelines than in the flatbed. But she was tired of living on the sidelines. Her whole life she'd been guarded by her overbearing relatives, who were always looking out for her. They never let her do anything fun. This could be her chance to make her own high school memories. A thrilling sensation seized her. Maybe she could even help her cousin win. Then he might let her hang out with him more often. Santiago's engine started up.

The truck made a wide circle, getting into position. Although she was nervous, it was also kind of thrilling to be in a race. She had forgotten all about finding a boyfriend. Santiago was going to get a big kick out of this, she thought.

A gunshot rang out into the air and Santiago's truck jumped into life. Alexis held her breath. The wind whipped the serape off her and it disappeared into the desert night.

The moon was especially bright. Over her shoulder she could make out the shape of the Salinas brothers' black Escalade racing along-side them. Just then, Santiago's truck kicked into a higher gear and accelerated ahead of the Escalade. This was the moment Alexis had been waiting for.

Travis Salinas was focused on the windy dirt road ahead of him. His brother, Brandon, started to poke him in the ribs.

"Bro," Travis cried in annoyance. "What's your problem?"

Brandon didn't utter a word. He gestured at the back of Santiago's truck.

Travis sighed and glanced at where his brother was pointing. He gasped and his eyes grew round at the sight of a dark apparition with a ghostly white face reaching out toward them. Both brothers screamed. Travis's leg pressed down on the brake and the Escalade spun to the right, barely missing Santiago's truck. The car whirled out of control until it finally crashed into a mesquite tree and stopped. Neither brother seemed hurt, but they both looked shaken up as they climbed out of their vehicle.

A few feet away, Santiago's truck came to an abrupt halt, throwing Alexis's body across the flatbed. She screamed. Santiago jumped out of the cab and ran a couple of feet toward the Salinas brothers' crash. When he registered Alexis's scream, he rushed back to his truck.

"Alexis! What the . . . ?"

"Surprise," Alexis said in a small voice. *This can't be good*, she thought, staring at the crash she'd caused. "I'm sorry. . . . I just wanted to slow them down. . . ."

Her cousin opened the tailgate and motioned for her to get out. "I can't believe this. . . . Do you know how bad this could have been?" Santiago wiped his brow, sweeping his soft curls out of his face. "Damn, girl." He let out a tight breath and leaned on the edge of the tailgate of his truck. "You scared the hell out of me."

"Sorry." Alexis's solemn face split into a grin. "You should have seen the look on Brandon's and Travis's faces, though. It was like they were seeing an actual ghost." She rubbed her face clean with the sleeves of her shirt.

Santiago couldn't help but smile. He swung his right arm around Alexis's neck and pulled her in a gentle headlock. With his left hand, he gave her a *coscorrón*. "That's for scaring me."

"Ouch!" Alexis cried, trying to push him away. "Hey, you can't treat me like that. Not after I helped you win. I want my ten percent."

Santiago released her and laughed. "We haven't won the race yet." He nodded down the road at a series of lights where the finish line had to be.

"Well, c'mon." Alexis pulled at his white T-shirt. "Let's go. What are we waiting for?"

"We?" Santiago shot her a stern look. "There ain't no 'we' here. I'm not even supposed to be here, you know? If your mother finds out . . ." His eyes bulged. "If my mother finds out . . ."

"I won't tell," Alexis cut in. "I promise. I can keep a secret."

Santiago twisted his lips into a frustrated scowl. He crossed his arms in front of his chest. "You want something, don't you?"

Alexis blushed. "I sorta kinda thought that maybe you could introduce me to some of your friends. . . ." she said, looking down at her dusty shoes. *Because you're supposed to introduce me to my new boyfriend*, Alexis added to herself.

Santiago shook his head. "No way. I don't want you talking to any of the fools out here tonight. You stick with me — and don't drink anything, you got it?"

"Ay, you're worse than Fabi," Alexis complained. "Oh, please, please, please." Alexis put her fingertips together in a praying gesture. "I just want to meet one guy. I promise I won't ask you to do another favor for me."

Brandon Salinas's voice interrupted them. "This is not over, Santiago! You cheated!"

Santiago jumped up and made his way to the front of his truck. Alexis rushed over to the passenger side and got in. He looked at her as he buckled his seat belt. "This stuff is dangerous. Didn't you just see what happened to Brandon and Travis back there? Not everyone comes out alive, you know."

He started the engine. The truck rolled toward the brilliant beams of the parked car lights at the finish line. Alexis watched wide-eyed as they entered the clearing. The crowd of onlookers rushed up to Santiago's truck, cheering loudly. Her cousin jumped out of the truck and into the arms of his adoring fans. Alexis took her time getting out. She searched through the crowd, not sure who she was actually looking for. Alexis breathed deeply. The air was cool and fresh. A country tune was playing behind her. A small flame ignited in the middle of her chest. Her destiny was here somewhere, she thought.

chapter 3

Alexis piled out of the yellow school bus along with a group of classmates in matching yellow-and-black Dos Rios High T-shirts. On this November morning, they were visiting the local university for the annual college day celebration. Alexis had signed up for the field trip because it got her out of school for the day. She didn't really have much interest in college. Her plan was to get a major recording contract before the age of seventeen. There were dozens of other high school buses from neighboring towns in the parking lot: Donna, McAllen,

Mission, Hidalgo, and Weslaco school districts. Alexis wondered how many cute single boys were also visiting the university today. She reached for the side pocket of her backpack, where she kept her makeup.

"Are you looking for a pen?" a gentle voice asked from behind her. Alexis turned to see the round face of Justin Peña.

"A pen?" he repeated, turning bright red. "I'm sure you want to take lots of notes. I hear it's very competitive to get into college nowadays."

Alexis stared at Justin as if he were speaking a foreign language. Why was he even talking to her, she wondered. Justin Peña was like a lost puppy that followed her home — which is exactly what he had done the first day of kindergarten. Alexis had hoped that he would grow out of his crush.

She gave Justin a tight smile. "I have a pen, thank you."

"Would you like some bottled water, or how about a —"

"Oh, look." Alexis pointed to the second Dos Rios High School bus that had pulled in behind them. Students were emptying out and gathering around Assistant Principal Castillo. "It's Santiago."

"Wasn't he a senior last year?" Justin asked, passing his hefty backpack to his other shoulder.

"Oh, yeah," Alexis answered absently. "He's on a five-year plan. All right, well, I'll see you later. Santi!" Alexis called out and rushed over to where her cousin was standing.

Justin hurried after her like a shadow. "I think we're all supposed to stay together," he said.

Alexis ignored him and tried to hide behind a group of girls that was standing next to Santiago. "Help me," Alexis whispered in a desperate tone.

Santiago smiled as he glanced over her shoulder at Justin. "I don't know why you don't give him a chance. My mom's always saying that dorky nerds in high school blossom into dorky rich swans after college. Ain't that right, Mr. Castillo?" Santiago turned to the assistant principal. "Were you a nerd in high school?"

The assistant principal gave Santiago a heated stare.

Santiago raised his arms in an "I give up" gesture. "Just kidding, man. Just kidding."

Alexis couldn't help but laugh. "What are you even doing here?"

"What?" Santiago placed his hands on his chest and shot her a disappointed look. "Just because I have to repeat senior year doesn't mean I can't have dreams, you know."

Alexis rolled her eyes.

"I'm part of the AP's 'special' list." Santiago emphasized the word "special" with his fingers. "The dude has a soft spot for knuckleheads like me and I love field trips. Plus, I always wanted to date a college girl." He nudged her in the ribs.

The group walked toward a series of white

tents in the middle of a large grassy area. Alexis had been to the university before, for a festival where lots of famous authors came and talked about their books. Alexis had given the free books she got to Chuy, the cook at her family's restaurant, so he could practice his English. She'd only gone so she could meet a real famous person. One day she would be like them, she told herself, signing autographs and taking pictures with fans.

"Hey, where's your sister?" Santiago asked, when they got to the registration table, where they each received a "Go to College" tote bag stuffed with university souvenirs. "She's the one who likes all this college stuff," he added, sticking a college bumper sticker from the bag on a passing girl's backpack.

Alexis shook her head. "Fabi said she couldn't miss class. She also said something about applying out of state. I don't know. Now that she's a junior, she's even more obsessed with her grades and work." Alexis rolled her eyes.

"Good thing I stuck around, huh?" Santiago joked, tying the rolled-up university bandanna around his forehead.

Alexis laughed, swatting at her cousin playfully.

The assistant principal called them over under a live oak. He proceeded to review the rules of conduct as if they were children. When Castillo mentioned the buddy system, she could feel Justin's stare on the back of her neck. Alexis inched closer to Santiago and hooked her arm into his before he could protest. A group of girls shot her dirty looks from across the circle, but she ignored them happily. As his cousin, she had first dibs. Blood was thicker than lipstick.

As a member of Castillo's "special" group, Santiago had to accompany AP Castillo to the workshops *he* had chosen specifically for *his* group. Alexis wanted to gag when they walked into a "financial awareness" workshop, until she realized that they were going to be talking about money. Out of the corner of her eye, she saw Justin sitting a safe distance away. Alexis wanted to scream. How was she supposed to find her future boyfriend with Justin dangling around like an old key chain?

When they broke for lunch under the tents, the Rio Grande Valley regional high school mariachi champions greeted them, strumming a potpourri of classic Mexican songs. Alexis was eager to check out the group. She hadn't competed the year before, because she was a freshman and still learning the songs. Last year's mariachi group was made up of mostly seniors, and they'd made it to the statewide semifinals in San Antonio. But when the music teacher switched to Roma High, a school with a better music program, Alexis's hopes for participating in the mariachi competitions were doused. She considered changing schools, but her parents refused. Without a music teacher, Alexis wondered if they'd even have a group this year. Mariachi was supposed to be her ticket to fame. Record scouts went to the high school competitions to find new talent. There was a girl from Sullivan City who was offered a record deal at last year's competition.

Alexis studied the musicians onstage. At first glance they didn't look like anything special. They were an all-female group, dressed in white mariachi greca-style two-piece suits with matching gold ties, sashes, and hair bows. *They must not have any good male musicians*, she thought.

Santiago elbowed her in the side. "What are you staring at?"

She nodded at the group. "They're supposed to be the best high school mariachi band in the Valley, but I don't see it."

Her cousin smiled. "I hear the lead singer is really good."

Alexis crossed her arms in front of her chest. As she glanced around, she caught sight of Justin Peña staring right at her. He waved, but Alexis sat down quickly on the grass, pretending not to notice him. Justin was in mariachi with her, too, but that didn't mean they needed to sit together for the concert. As the intro continued, she craned her neck to see around the stage. Where was this big-shot singer?

Suddenly, from nowhere and everywhere, a melodious voice rang out from the speakers. The voice struck her like an arrow.

The source of the voice stepped into view. He was gorgeous, Alexis thought, admiring his dark hair, flirtatious smile, and beautiful brown eyes. The singer was dressed all in black except for a small red rose pinned to his jacket. There were horse-shaped silver buttons on his coat and down the side of his polyester-wool-blend pants. He held a wide-brimmed sombrero in one hand and a wireless mic in the other.

Is this a dream? Alexis wondered as the figure floated by her. He was so close she could have brushed his leg with her hand. She realized with a start that he looked like the guy she had seen in the Salinas brothers' car the other night. She couldn't be sure, though.

The singer paused on his way to the stage and took an audience member's hand, delicately pressing it to his lips. Everyone — or to be more precise, all the girls under the canopy — went wild.

The crowd jumped up and rushed forward as the singer took the stage. If only she had sat closer to the stage. There was no way she could possibly catch his attention from all the way in the back. Who was this guy? How come she'd never heard of him — or how gorgeous he was?

"Oh, no," Santiago groaned. "Not you, too. You're all gaga for El Charro Negro, aren't you? You and all the girls here." He glanced at the audience members cheering and crying out to the singer. "How am I supposed to compete with this dude? I can't even carry a tune," he joked.

"Is that his name?" Alexis asked. She wanted to know everything about him. "The Black Horseman. Is it because he has a dark soul? Or maybe some girl broke his heart and now he doesn't believe that he can ever love again. I'm right, aren't I?"

"Chill out, *cousin*." Santiago grinned, shaking his head. "Don't let your fantasies run away with you. I think they call him that because he only wears black. He must think it makes him look mysterious . . . like Zorro. I think it's kinda stupid."

"You're just jealous," Alexis cried, slapping him on the chest. "You just don't get artistic types. We're mysterious people, okay? Regular people just can't understand us."

"Us?"

"Yes. Us. I'm an artist, too, you know."

Santiago's face opened up into a gigantic, cheeky smile.

"Don't make that face. I'm going to be a famous singer someday. I'll have tons of fans, you'll see."

Santiago nodded, raising his index finger. "Well, for now you have one adoring fan, just one." He gestured to where Justin was still lurking, off to the side.

"Oh, shut up." Alexis was losing her patience with Santiago. She moved up, determined to catch El Charro Negro's eye. As an artist, she knew how tough this business was — surely they had a lot in common. Maybe they would become fast friends — or maybe something more? Could it be possible that he was the dark man the old lady from the *botánica* told her about? *He must be!* she thought. Didn't her cousin lead her to him? Alexis checked her face in her compact. She pinched her cheeks to make them rosy and dabbed on some lip gloss. Then she walked toward the stage.

Alexis didn't get very far, however. Not one girl would let her through the crowd. She glanced over her shoulder and noticed her cousin grinning from ear to ear. There was no way she could go back.

Over in the far corner, to the left of the stage, she noticed a woman in a red business suit talking on a cell phone. She leaned on the metal railing that separated the musicians and stage crew from the hungry-eyed audience. *That must be the event coordinator or his manager*, Alexis thought, making her way over to her. El Charro would probably pass her on his way out.

Alexis waited as he sang several heartfelt ballads. Her heart beat wildly. He was so talented. Hearing the familiar mariachi songs sung by El Charro felt like hearing them for the first time. She wanted to grab each word he sang and lock it away in a safe for only her to hear.

Finally, he finished. Alexis felt like she'd been awakened rudely from a blissful dream. *Is that really it?* El Charro Negro pulled the red rose from his lapel and threw it into the audience. It seemed like every girl under the canopy dove for the flower.

But then he was gone. She turned suddenly, looking for El Charro Negro. Alexis sighed with relief when he walked up to the woman in red — just like she'd guessed. The woman thanked him with a big hug. Surprised, the boy jerked back, right into the metal gate — and right into Alexis.

He turned to apologize, but Alexis seized her opportunity. "Hi, my name is Alexis. I saw your performance just now. You're pretty good. I sing as well. I play the violin, too." She felt herself babbling, but couldn't stop.

El Charro Negro glanced at her with a perplexed look in his dark eyes. Suddenly, Alexis felt the metal gate shake and heard a girl yell, "He's over here!"

The mob was getting out of control. Alexis thought quickly. "I know a way to get you out of here," she said urgently. He nodded, so she grabbed the *charro* by the wrist and started to run. The screams from the mob rang in her ears. Her heart pounded loudly in her chest. Alexis ran as fast as she could, weaving in and out across the grassy school landscape, around college students, trees, and benches. She finally stopped behind a big school building, out of breath. Panting loudly next to her was El Charro Negro. Alexis did a double take to make sure she wasn't dreaming. He was so cute, even in his disheveled state. Just as she had that thought, he looked up at her. His warm chocolate eyes locked with hers and made her stomach quiver with anticipation.

"Wow, that was close. Thanks for helping me," he said, wiping his forehead.

Alexis beamed. "Don't worry about it. Saving *charros* from a mob of adoring fans is a hobby of mine."

The boy smiled. "Really?"

Alexis shrugged. "It's a gift."

"Then maybe I should have you around more often."

Alexis's heart skipped a beat.

"Last month, at the Brownsville County Fair, a sixty-year-old woman ripped off my shoe while I was singing."

Alexis laughed.

Suddenly, a white van pulled up alongside them. A man with a big mustache motioned for El Charro Negro to get in. Alexis noticed a couple of the girls from the mariachi band packed in the backseat like sardines. The *charro* smiled at the driver as he jumped into the front seat. Alexis hung back by the wall, not sure what to do next. Should she ask for a ride? Should she give him her number?

"Hey," El Charro Negro called out to her from the van.

Alexis looked up at him, her heart soaring with joy.

"Thanks again," he said, and waved goodbye as the van pulled away.

Alexis stood by the curb and watched the van disappear into traffic. *He's the one!* Excitement started to shoot up from her toes. Alexis couldn't hold it back any longer. She screamed at the top of her lungs. This had been the best day ever!

chapter 4

On Monday, Alexis combed through the local papers online at the school library for any information about her *charro*. Alexis started a list in her history notebook of things she learned about him.

<u>Things I Know:</u>

1. Name: Christian Luna ♥ ♥
2. Junior at Performing Arts High School
3. Won best male singer award at the Rodeo Exposition in Corpus Christi last year

4. Handsome ♥

5. Amazing singer

<u>Things I Don't Know:</u>

1. Does he like me?

2. Does he have a girlfriend?

3. Does he like me?

4. What's his favorite song?

5. Does he like me? ☺

The sixth-period bell rang, waking Alexis from her thoughts. It was time for mariachi practice, and she couldn't help but be nervous. Ever since Mr. Fernandez left the Dos Rios mariachi ensemble, they'd had a string of unqualified teachers. Now it was the assistant principal's turn. Alexis feared that if he didn't work out, the school might just scrap the program altogether.

Alexis took a deep breath and walked down the hallway toward the storage room. When they lost their music teacher, they also lost their nice music studio. With no one to fight on their behalf, they were left sharing a space with the janitorial staff.

Nikki was waiting for her by the girls' bathroom. Her *guitarrón*, a large bass guitar, was strapped over her shoulder with a pink sash. The thing was so big, Alexis always worried that Nikki would tip over from the weight.

Nikki was chewing on the tip of her braid. "Do you think Castillo will work out?" she asked. Alexis shrugged as she opened the door that led to the storage room. "I hate practicing here," Nikki added in a low voice. "It's so cold and depressing."

The storage room had been rearranged for their arrival. Broken desks, mops, and brooms had been pushed to the side to make room for a semicircle of chairs and black music stands. Alexis noted a few new faces. Castillo had warned her that he was adding new members to the group. So many seniors had graduated last year that they were left with only three continuing musicians. In order to compete, they had to have at least eight people. But these new members had to be some kind of joke, Alexis thought.

She counted seven new bodies. Three were dozing off. One girl with a ton of makeup and big reddish hair was chatting loudly on her cell phone. In the back, a scary-looking girl in black sat reading a comic book. Two thug-looking types were scratching their names onto metal chairs. *Oh, no*, Alexis realized. *This is AP Castillo's "special" group.*

"Hi," Justin said behind her. Alexis jumped. "Looks like we'll have a full ensemble now." He was holding his trumpet case and smiling.

Alexis wanted to wipe the smile off his face. "Justin, are you serious? Look at them. They're not musicians. They're hoodlums."

"Who you callin' hoodlums, *fresa*?" the girl on the cell phone snapped, closing her phone and slipping it into the pocket of her supertight jeans. She stood and got right up in Alexis's face. This close, Alexis noticed that she was wearing violet-colored contacts. It made her look a little alien-like with her red-streaked hair and brown skin.

Alexis glanced around, wondering if anyone was going to step in. The tough girl was about her height, but she looked mean, like she probably fought dirty.

Suddenly, the door opened, interrupting their argument. A man yelled, "Get in there right now." Alexis recognized AP Castillo's voice and sighed with relief. The assistant principal would realize his mistake and take these guys somewhere else to serve detention. But when Alexis turned around, she was surprised to see her cousin Santiago coming through the door with a frown on his face.

"Santi," Alexis cried. "What on earth are you doing here?"

Before Santiago could say anything, AP

Castillo slapped him on the back. "He's the newest member of the Dos Rios mariachi ensemble. Isn't that right, Santiago?"

Santiago squirmed a bit under the AP's firm stare. He finally relented. "Yes, sir."

Confused, Alexis looked to AP Castillo. "I don't understand. None of these guys play instruments."

AP Castillo smiled, revealing his clear braces. There was a strange gleam in his hazel eyes. "I figure mariachi is exactly what these guys need. This music is all about taking pride in one's culture — and the practices will be good to build discipline."

Alexis doubled over as if socked in the stomach. Was he intentionally trying to sabotage their chances of competing? Alexis looked from Nikki to Justin for help.

"It'll be fun," Castillo continued as he pulled out a guitar from the closet. "Besides, you need more members and these students need an activity — it's perfect!"

"I didn't know you played the guitar," Nikki said, perking up a bit.

"I don't." He laughed. "But I've been watching some YouTube videos, and I figure we can all start at the beginning together."

Alexis felt her dreams slip between her fingertips. Now how was she supposed to compete at the statewide competition and get discovered by a music scout?

A few days later, Alexis and Santiago went to her family's restaurant together after practice. She didn't understand how Santiago had done it, but he had convinced AP Castillo to let him play the accordion. As far as she could remember, Santiago had never shown any interest in their late grandfather's music. Now he wouldn't stop jabbering about how this was going to connect him to his roots and how he was having these dreams where their grandfather, Lil Rafa, came to him, blah blah blah. Alexis pushed open the door, welcoming the comforting sounds of a Northern Mexican ballad playing on the old jukebox.

Her mother, Magda, bussed tables and scolded someone on the cordless phone. "How come whenever a big concert is in town, you two get sick all of a sudden? No. Wasn't your mamá ill last week? Your poor mamá is always sick. Maybe I should bring her some chicken soup." Magda motioned for Alexis and Santiago to get out of her way with a flick of her wrist.

In the kitchen, Alexis heard pots and pans clanging. Chuy, her dad's right-hand man, was rushing around the kitchen. He had taken on more responsibilities after her dad's minor heart attack six months ago. The heart attack brought the family together. Everyone wanted to do their part to help with the ever-growing medical bills — Alexis had stopped taking private vocal lessons.

Turning to her left, she admired the wall-high shrine to her late grandfather, Lil Rafa "Los Dedos del Valle" Treviño Garza. The shrine was decorated with burning candles, incense, fake flowers, tequila, his famous accordion, and other trinkets her grandmother Trini had collected.

Alexis noticed Santiago talking to their grandmother Trini. He motioned to the accordion. Grandma Trini sat at a table she'd converted into a Lil Rafa souvenir stand — complete with CDs, miniature replicas of her late husband, bumper stickers, and the crochet doilies she made herself.

Alexis's dad, Leonardo, was also with Grandma Trini. Walking up to them, she noticed that her dad was crocheting a toilet seat cover. Leonardo had taken up crochet while he was in recovery to help him relax, and soon realized that he was really good at it. Her dad looked up as she approached.

Leonardo held up the toilet seat cover for her to admire. "What do you think?"

"It's beautiful, Dad," Alexis said, touching the intricate weave.

Suddenly, Leonardo sniffed the air. His eyes grew large with alarm. He passed the crochet piece to Grandma Trini and stood up. "Chuy," he growled.

"Sorry! Sorry!" Chuy cried from the kitchen in Spanish. Moments later, Chuy appeared carrying a big silver pot, his straight black hair held back with a hairnet. He was a small guy with sharp eyes and an easy smile. "Sorry! Sorry!" he repeated as he carried the pot of burnt beans out the back door.

Alexis turned her attention back to her grandma Trini and Santiago. Grandma Trini was reaching into the altar to grab the accordion. Alexis watched in horror as her cousin put the instrument on upside down. Trini giggled and showed him how to put it on correctly.

Santiago combed his fingers through his locks and began pushing random buttons as he tried to sing "La Bamba." His voice was totally off-key, but Grandma Trini didn't seem to notice. She was clapping for him like he was a rock star. Thankfully, Santiago left after one song to serenade the other customers.

"Smell me," Trini commanded, thrusting her voluptuous boobs at Alexis's face.

Alexis took a sniff and made a curious face. "What am I smelling?"

Trini licked her pink lips and glanced around the room. "I was reading this article about male pheromones I borrowed from the doctor's office—"

"Stole! You stole that magazine!" Alexis's other grandmother, Abuelita Alpha, cried from her side of the restaurant. The two grandmothers were always meddling in each other's business. *Mentirosa.*

Trini leaned into Alexis. "Anyway, like I was saying," she said. "They makes the men hungry for love," she explained. "So I got some of the used bacon lard from the kitchen to test it out. What do you think?"

Alexis winced at the thought. "I don't know, Grandma."

"Here you go, honey," her mother interrupted, placing a plate of quesadillas with rice and beans in front of Alexis. It was her favorite meal.

Alexis stared at the plate. She couldn't imagine eating anything at the moment. All she could think about were her doused dreams, the dysfunctional mariachi group, and El Charro Negro. She had done everything the old lady told her to do. Her chest tightened at the thought of never singing with El Charro Negro onstage. "I'm sorry, but I'm not hungry."

"Not hungry!" both grandmothers cried out together.

Abuelita Alpha stormed across the room in her favorite black dress. Usually she respected Trini's side of the restaurant, but this was an emergency. Alpha put a cold, pruned palm on Alexis's forehead. "She doesn't have a fever."

"But look at those bags," Trini cried.

"I think she looks sad." Her mother frowned.

"Where does it hurt?" Alpha asked, poking Alexis's shoulder.

Alexis shrugged. "I don't know, all over, I guess."

Her grandmothers and mother cried out in anguish.

"She's lovesick," Trini explained to a customer who looked shocked by their outburst. "We Garzas are very passionate women, you know."

"There is a boy I like," Alexis began. "He sings mariachi at the new performing arts high school in Mission. You know, the one I wanted to go to." Her mother and grandmothers nodded with understanding. Alexis felt her chest tighten again as she continued. "And to make it worse, our high school mariachi group totally sucks this year. I'll never be able to compete at his level and he'll never look at me."

"Ay, *mija*," her mother said in a comforting voice. "I'm sorry things are not as you planned.

But maybe you're just looking at it wrong. Have you even tried to woo him?"

"Have you no shame!" Abuelita Alpha cried, making the sign of the cross over her chest. "A decent woman would never chase after a man."

"Sometimes they need a little help," her mother said. "Your dad was so shy. I thought he would never ask me out."

"Really?" Alexis couldn't believe her ears. "What happened?"

"Well." Her mother sat down. Her eyes twinkled with a hint of mischief. "I asked *him* out. He tried to hide from me at first, but I didn't give up. I knew that he was the one and I was not going to let him go without a fight."

Abuelita Alpha frowned as she patted her daughter's hand. "You never told me that. I always thought he chased you. This is all my fault. I should have let you curl your eyelashes when you wanted — then maybe you wouldn't have turned out so unladylike."

Trini rolled her eyes and then turned to Alexis. "So you see, sometimes boys are a little slow."

Alexis's mom smiled. "Sometimes?"

"Most times," Trini corrected herself. "You can't just give up. You make him notice you. Once he sees you, he has no choice but to fall madly in love with you."

"But how am I supposed to do that? He goes to school in Mission. I don't know where he lives. He might have a girlfriend — or maybe ten." Alexis swallowed her growing anxiety.

Trini handed Alexis a bacon-scented handkerchief that she had been keeping tucked in her bosom. *"No hay peor lucha que la que no se hace."* Alexis gave her a confused look and Trini translated: "The worst fight is the one not taken . . . or something like that."

Suddenly, there was the sound of breaking glass. Her father started cursing. Alexis was about to run into the kitchen when she heard her dad yell: "What idiot put an upside-down candle of San Antonio in my oven?" Alexis blushed and sat back down to eat her plate of food in silence.

chapter 5

Alexis was not surprised when none of AP Castillo's "special" students showed up for practice the next day. Justin started setting up the chairs as if they were just running late. Alexis pulled out her phone to call her cousin. Santiago was probably hanging out with a new girlfriend. She was about to tell Justin to forget about the others when Nikki raced into the room with her large *guitarrón* case.

"Castillo is out looking for people," Nikki said, out of breath. "He asked us to help."

"What are we supposed to do?" Alexis cried, throwing her arms in the air. "Calf rope them and drag them back?"

Justin laughed.

Alexis shook her head. "Forcing those guys to take mariachi was a big mistake."

Nikki set her *guitarrón* down by a chair. "Don't be like that," Nikki said, grabbing Alexis's hand and pulling her out of the room. Justin followed at her heels. "We need them. You know we do."

Alexis sighed inwardly. She hated when her friend was right. They walked down the deserted hallways searching for the missing mariachi members in empty classrooms, behind stairways, and around columns. In the girls' bathroom, Alexis saw the scary girl's black combat boots in the last stall. Justin decided to wait outside.

Alexis walked up to the door and pounded on it.

"Go away!" the scary girl said.

Alexis took a breath. She glanced at Nikki for support. Nikki mouthed the words "Be nice" at Alexis.

"Excuse me," Alexis said, trying to make her voice calm.

"This stall is busy," the girl said in a stern voice.

Alexis wanted to kick down the door. She wanted to tell the girl to just forget about mariachi, but Nikki was right. They needed a full mariachi ensemble, and no one else had auditioned. She had to bring AP Castillo's group of misfits together. "I'm sorry to bother you. My name is Alexis. I'm in the mariachi group. The group that's supposed to be meeting right now."

Silence.

"Well . . . I just wanted to see if maybe you'd like to try out the violin. I've been playing it for a while and we could practice together. If you want . . ."

The stall door flew open. Alexis jumped back, narrowly missing getting hit. The scary girl still didn't say a word; she just stared at Alexis through black eyeglass frames. Alexis wondered if she was going to bite her.

"You want to teach me?" the girl asked in disbelief.

Alexis felt her cheeks flush. "Well, yeah, that's if you want to learn. You don't have to play the violin. I just thought it would be cool to have two people play violin in the group." Alexis searched the girl's pale face. She couldn't read her expression, especially not behind her nest of messy, dyed-black hair.

"I thought you didn't want us in your group," the girl said.

"We do," Nikki cut in. Alexis was grateful for the backup.

"Yeah," Alexis tried again. "We actually need you. If you're willing to give us a shot."

The girl was silent again for a moment, glancing from Nikki to Alexis and back again. Then she shrugged. "I guess it beats picking up trash."

"Yay!" Alexis cheered.

"I'm Marisol, by the way."

"I'm Alexis and this is Nikki," Alexis responded. The scary girl had a name. It was a good first step. Alexis grabbed Marisol's hand and pulled her out of the bathroom. "Let's go see if we can round up some more recruits."

They found the *cholo* twins tagging the back of the library wall. Alexis had to threaten to call the cops before they decided to come along. Pedro and Pablo were actually pretty harmless, Alexis thought, once you got over their tough-guy exteriors and clown-sized baggy clothes. As they circled around the outside of the cafeteria, Justin noticed something.

"Hey" — he pointed across the lawn — "isn't that the rude girl with the cell phone?"

They all looked and noticed her walking across the grassy lawn with an unlit cigarette hanging off her lower lip. Before Alexis could say anything, the group took off to go after her.

"Wait up," Alexis yelled after them.

The rude girl spotted them coming from twenty feet away and shouted: "I'm not joining your stupid band, so leave me alone."

"Please just give it a chance," Nikki said as she approached.

"No," the girl snapped, crossing her arms in front of her chest. "You can't make me."

The thug twins smirked at each other. "Wanna bet, Karina?" they said to the rude girl in unison. The taller twin spoke up. "But for real, you know Castillo. He's not going to let up. This mariachi stuff is better than Castillo's boot camp training and those ugly orange uniforms he made us wear. I'll do whatever it takes to keep from wearing that uniform again."

Karina's eyes got really big as the brothers came near her. She took a step back. "You better stop!" Her voice sounded nervous. "Don't come any closer."

Karina glanced around for an escape. Then she took off running to the football field. That's when everyone started to run. Karina began yelling at the top of her lungs as she looped around the grassy lawn. She was quick and spun right out of the twins' clutches. This was crazy, Alexis thought. Then she noticed Karina running in her direction. She was too focused on the boys behind her to look forward. Alexis screamed, "Stop!" just as Karina slammed right into her.

The force of the collision threw both girls back onto the grass. Alexis reached for her forehead. There was sure to be a bruise. Karina cried out as she rubbed at the top of her head. The two girls stared at each other. All of a sudden, Karina started to giggle. Then her giggle turned into a loud, full-bellied laugh. Alexis couldn't help but laugh with her. Then everyone started cracking up. She noted the smiling faces around her. Maybe they could become a group after all? Karina got up, cleaned the pieces of grass off her jeans, and then offered Alexis a hand. Alexis hesitated. There was a small smile creeping onto Karina's lips.

"I can't believe you guys want me in your mariachi group. Have you heard me play that stringy thing?" She crossed her eyes and made a crazy face. "You must be really desperate for members. I don't get it. Why do you guys care so much?"

Alexis blinked, stunned. They were desperate. But this was a highly unusual situation. Most schools had waiting lists for their mariachi groups. People had to audition to even be considered. Mariachi was a prestigious school activity — just not at Dos Rios. If only she could find the right words to show Karina and the rest of the group how great high school mariachi could be.

"Yes, we are desperate," Justin said, coming up behind Alexis. "We want to form a group. We want to perform. We do care and we're not ashamed to admit it. Mariachi music is more than just singing love songs at restaurants."

Alexis stared at Justin. He looked taller, more confident standing there. She couldn't help but feel proud.

"Mariachi music is powerful. It can bring people to their knees. When I play my trumpet, I feel the song coursing in me," he continued. "Our music is who we are — it's in our blood. I feel like I can do anything when I play."

Everyone stared at Justin. No one dared laugh. The gleam in his brown eyes told them that he was speaking his truth. His words moved Alexis. She wondered if his speech was enough to sway the new recruits.

When no one said anything, Alexis said, "I have an idea. Do you guys want to see something?"

The group exchanged glances and then nodded.

They drove to the new performing arts academy, located in the city of Mission. On the way,

Alexis explained the world of competitive high school mariachi. The way it usually worked was that each school ensemble would go head-to-head against other schools in their district and then move up to compete statewide and even nationally, if they were really good. There were cash prizes for best male singer, best female singer, and best group ensemble — and of course the bragging rights that came with these titles. Some contestants had even been offered record contracts after the tournament. Every year there were rumors of sabotage or cheating, so schools fiercely guarded their teams and performance secrets.

Pedro, the tall lanky twin, whistled when they walked onto the campus. The high school looked more like a college, with its numerous state-of-the-art buildings and perfectly manicured lawns. This was the arts magnet school that Alexis had wanted to apply to, but their waiting list was ridiculous.

"You sure it's okay if we're here?" Marisol asked. Alexis turned back to face her.

"Well, technically you guys aren't in mariachi yet, so we're not competition." Alexis smiled in a flirty way. "This is just a field trip."

The group nodded approvingly. She led them to a modern-looking building with south-facing windows that curved into a semicircle. Alexis's heart started to beat wildly as they climbed the steps. She had a secret agenda. Only Nikki knew, because she was her best friend. Christian Luna, aka "El Charro Negro," went to this school. Alexis was secretly hoping to see him, or better yet, actually talk to him.

Mariachi music poured out of the main concert hall. In the lobby there was a wall-length glass case filled with gold trophies and photos of the high school mariachi regional champions. In the middle of the group was Christian Luna, wearing his signature black outfit. Her heart skipped a beat. But this was no time to swoon over him, she told herself. She was here to inspire her would-be mariachis. Alexis motioned for them to be silent and the group tiptoed to a door that seemed to lead to the auditorium. It was locked.

"Tough security," Karina commented, snapping her gum loudly.

Pablo, the short twin, studied the lock. He glanced at his brother, who nodded in understanding. Alexis stared wide-eyed at Nikki when she realized that they were going to pick the lock. *Who are these guys?* Alexis wondered, glancing around the lobby. Pedro passed Pablo a set of silver keys and a small screwdriver. Pablo inserted a key and pounded it in with the back of the screwdriver. Alexis jumped at the sound. Thankfully, the music inside concealed the click of the door unlocking. Alexis held her breath. She thought about backing out. *We've already gone this far*, she thought as she led the group into the darkened auditorium.

The group huddled by the door, camouflaged by the darkness. Bright floodlights illuminated the professional concert stage. Alexis's heart swelled. She dreamed of one day singing in a fancy auditorium like this. Onstage, a group of musicians dressed in their school uniforms stood at attention listening to the music director. It was a twenty-piece ensemble with six violins, one *guitarrón*, five trumpet players, a harpist, four guitarists, and three students holding small guitars called *vihuelas*. Alexis gasped at the sheer size of the entire group. This was way more people than had been a part of the university show.

Suddenly, the sound of violins filled the auditorium. Then a sweet melody from the trumpets joined the violins. Alexis felt consumed by the music. She glanced at her teammates and noticed the look of rapture in their eyes. *They really like it!* Alexis thought happily. Alexis's heart skipped when a familiar voice rose to join the melody. It was Christian! She didn't recognize the song, but she could tell that it was fun and flirty by the way he moved across the stage. When the song ended, Alexis heard her group sigh. She smiled. They were hooked.

Then her cell phone rang. She'd downloaded a mariachi ringtone onto her phone just last week. Now that crazy song was filling up the whole room — and drawing unwanted attention to their presence. The musicians onstage all turned in her direction. The music director shouted:

"Who's over there?"

Alexis's heart leapt into her throat. The phone was still ringing and she couldn't get it to stop.

"Spies! I knew we'd get spies," the director cried, throwing his music sheets in the air. "Will someone get the lights and hunt those people down?"

Someone grabbed Alexis's hand and pulled her out of the darkened hall. It was Justin. They all hurried out of the building, down the stairs, and across the lawn, not looking back. Alexis's pulse was racing. They could not get caught, she thought. The group would be banned from ever performing and she could kiss all her dreams good-bye. Luckily, no one seemed to have followed them out into the parking lot.

Her phone rang again. Alexis looked at the number. It was Santiago. She was going to kill him.

"Yo, Alexis, where you at?" Santiago asked casually. "Castillo's been looking for you. He's pretty ticked off. He thinks you ditched mariachi practice."

Alexis gasped. In her rush to show the group a real mariachi performance, she had totally forgotten about AP Castillo. "Tell Castillo I'm sorry. I took the group on a field trip."

"Field trip? And you didn't invite me?" Santiago said, sounding hurt. "Hey, listen to this," Santiago said, putting down the phone. She glanced at the group catching their breath around her. They were giving her curious looks. Before she could say anything, garbled wheezing tones came out from the other end of the phone. It was painful to hear. It sounded like a dying mule crying out in pain. There was a pause and then Santiago came back on the phone. "So . . . what do you think?"

Alexis noted the excitement in his voice. "Not bad," she lied. "Keep practicing."

"I will," Santiago said. "I think I have a knack for this thing. Like it's in my blood, or something."

Alexis thought back to what Justin said about mariachi music being in their veins, and smiled. "Yeah, I think it is."

The group split into the two carloads they'd come in, promising to meet for practice the following day. Alexis lingered a bit in the school parking lot, not wanting to leave. This was her chance to study Christian. She could find out what he did after practice. Did he have a job? Or a girlfriend he walked home?

"Hey, *fresa*, forget something?"

"My name's not *fresa*! It's Alexis. I hate it when you call me *fresa*, okay?" Alexis spat, spinning around quickly. Karina flinched, turning red. She was sitting behind the wheel of a dark blue Ford Bronco monster truck. Marisol and Nikki stared from inside the car, surprised by Alexis's reaction. Alexis blushed.

"Sorry. I didn't mean to bite your head off. I was just . . . I was thinking about . . ."

"She's waiting for a guy," Nikki blurted.

Alexis shot her best friend a heated stare. How dare she reveal her secret in front of these strangers?

Karina's violet eyes lit up. "Boy stalking is my specialty. Hop in." She motioned with her hand.

The girls rearranged themselves so that Alexis could sit in the front. *Corrido* music was playing on the radio. Karina explained that it was an original *narcocorrido*, a popular northern ballad–style of music that focused on the activities of drug dealers, including beheadings, burning houses, and shootings. This song was written for her boyfriend. He was a *narco*, Karina bragged. Alexis knew that *narco* was short for "drug dealer." Alexis liked the danceable polka-like beat despite the gruesome song lyrics. The singer's voice sounded familiar. She wondered if she'd heard the song on the radio before.

Alexis forgot about the *narcocorrido* when Nikki squealed at the sight of the musicians coming out of the music building. She studied each student as they walked down the steps. What if Christian stayed late or slipped out another door? Then she spotted him walking alone.

"That's him! That's him!" Alexis cried.

"Qué chulo," Karina admired.

Alexis jerked as if she'd been hit with a jealous stick. Karina noticed.

"Don't worry, Alexis. I have a boyfriend, remember?"

Alexis's cheeks flushed. She felt so childish as she mumbled an apology. Karina gestured for her to forget about it.

"He won best male singer last year," Nikki commented from the backseat.

Suddenly, Alexis noticed that Christian was heading straight toward them. "Duck down! Duck down!" she hissed as Christian passed right in front of their truck. He hurried through the parking lot and disappeared behind a car. Her heart beat wildly. "Do you think he saw us?"

"I doubt it," Nikki said, grinning. "So . . . now what?"

Alexis turned and gave Karina a knowing glance.

"Now this is what I call fun," Karina said as she pulled into traffic. Alexis couldn't help but be impressed with Karina's boy-stalking technique. They followed Christian from a discreet distance down the street, and then for another five blocks. Finally, he headed straight into an older four-plex apartment building. Alexis noticed the gang signs spray-painted on the ground-floor wall. Then she looked at the teenage boys in front of the complex drinking and playing rap music from a car.

"So . . ." Karina said, tapping her manicured nails on the steering wheel. "We could try to climb to the window for a peek."

Alexis blushed. "Really? Have you done that before?" Karina was bold and gutsy. Alexis couldn't help but like her.

Nikki nudged her from behind. "Go find out which apartment he lives in."

Alexis shook her head. "But what if he sees me? I don't want him to think I'm a crazy stalker or anything."

"Well, you kind of are," Nikki said in a teasing way. "But so what? I think it's romantic. Besides, don't you want to go see which apartment is his? I know I would."

Nikki was cut short by the sound of a door slamming shut. Alexis jerked back and noticed that scary girl Marisol was no longer in the car. She watched in horror as Marisol crept toward the apartment complex like a black cat.

"Wait!" Alexis yelled. Karina started to laugh. "What's she doing?" Alexis asked.

Nikki hushed her. "Let her go."

Marisol crossed the driveway. The boys in front of the complex called out to her, making kissing sounds. But Marisol must have shot them one of her scary-girl looks, because they shut up. Marisol went up to the second floor. Alexis's heart thumped wildly as she watched her move toward the door Christian had entered just moments ago. She couldn't see very well from inside the car and thought about getting out. But just as suddenly, Marisol was rushing back down the stairs.

She jumped into the car just as the door on the second floor opened and an older woman in a floral dress and short hair stepped onto the porch.

"Drive," Marisol said, out of breath.

Karina turned on the ignition and sped down the street. The girls screamed as they rode away.

"Did you see anything?" Alexis cried, turning to Marisol in the backseat.

A small smile danced on Marisol's lips. "He lives in apartment number four."

chapter 6

Alexis twirled a pencil in her hand as she tried to decide what to do. She stared across the table at Nikki, who was struggling over her Geometry worksheet. The two friends often did their homework together at the Garza family restaurant. *Stop procrastinating*, Alexis scolded herself. Nikki probably thought she was doing her Geometry, too. But Alexis was actually grappling over a letter to Christian she'd been unsuccessfully trying to write for the past half hour.

She wanted Christian to like her, but she wasn't sure how to make that happen. It had been so much easier with her previous boyfriends. Boys had always seemed to like her. Well, they used to. Now she was the one doing the pursuing. Who knew writing a love letter would be so hard?

Nikki glanced up and noticed Alexis's frustration. "What's wrong?"

"Oh, nothing," Alexis lied and glanced around the room. Her family's restaurant was bustling with customers, loud Mexican music, and busy waitstaff. Her sister walked by, balancing several plates of delicious-smelling food. Her stomach rumbled. "Fabi," she cried out, "we're hungry."

"Get up and serve yourself, then," her sister barked.

Just then, Nikki snatched Alexis's letter from her hands. "What's this?" Nikki asked.

"It's nothing," Alexis said, lunging across the table to get the letter back.

Nikki pulled back and read aloud, "'Dear Chris. Can I call you Chris?'"

Alexis glanced around the restaurant, hoping no one in her family could hear. Her ears burned fiery hot. She couldn't believe Nikki! Her friend continued reading. "'I'm the girl who saved you from the mob at the college fair. I just wanted to write you a letter and say . . .'" Nikki stopped and looked up at Alexis. "Say what? That I *loooooooove* you?"

Alexis got ahold of the paper and ripped it. "Hey, that's personal."

"What's personal?" her grandma Trini asked, coming up to their table and patting her new updo. Trini's dark hair was teased up in a messy bun with ringlets framing her heart-shaped face. Trini noticed the torn paper in both girls' hands. She pulled a chair from another table and joined them.

"What did you say to her?" Abuelita Alpha scolded as she crossed the room. "Those children have innocent ears. Don't be telling them any stories about going to the Island for Spring Break."

Trini flinched and her cheeks reddened. "I said nothing of the sort. For being such a good Catholic, you sure have a dirty mind." That shut Alpha up.

Alexis sat up. She had to squash the dispute before it got out of hand. "Fine! I'll tell you. But you have to promise to not fight." She waited until both old ladies nodded. "I was just writing a letter to the boy I have a crush on. But every time I try, it just sounds so dumb." She gestured to the crumpled papers littering the table surface.

"No, you're going about it all wrong," Alpha said, pulling out her rosary from her brassiere. "What you should do is get down and pray to San Antonio."

I've already tried that, Alexis thought.

"A love letter." Trini clapped her hands, ignoring Alpha. "We'd love to help."

Alpha stopped praying and looked at Trini sideways. "What do you mean 'we'?"

"Of course it should be us," Trini said, placing her hand on her bosom. "We are the matrons of the family, and it is our duty to train our granddaughter in the art of *el amor*."

Alexis glanced at Nikki. She was grinning ear to ear. Alexis couldn't resist smiling in response, a glimmer of hope fluttering in her chest. Maybe they could help. She picked up her pen and prepared to write.

"Okay, *mija*, take this down word for word," Trini said, twirling a ringlet with her finger as she thought. Trini took a deep breath and sang in a passionate voice: "Hey there, tall, dark, and handsome. When you pass by, my knees go weak and my heart whirls in a sweet dream. I long to kiss those lips, touch your skin, and breathe you into my soul . . ."

"That's a song!" Nikki cried.

Trini blushed and rested a hand to her

heart. "I can't help it if everything I learned about love is from the radio."

"Those are horrible lyrics." Alpha shook her head in disgust. "You could have at least chosen a happy song."

"Song?" Nikki said, her eyes growing round. "That's it!" Nikki grabbed Alexis's hand. "Don't write, sing."

"Sing him a letter?" Alexis asked, glancing from Nikki to her grandmothers.

"Oh, yes." Trini batted her eyes. "A *serenata* would be so much better than a stupid love letter. The *serenata* is truly romantic. It's part of our culture, our heritage. In the movies it's always a guy who comes to a girl's window at night to confess his feelings for her." Trini's eyes sparkled as she sighed. "Then the girl turns on the lights and comes onto her balcony to show the boy that she likes him, too."

"I must agree with your grandma Trini," Abuelita Alpha said in a grave voice. "No one can resist a *serenata*. It takes real guts to sing your heart out in front of the whole world." She glanced sideways at Grandpa Frank sitting at the opposite end of the counter with a bunch of his buddies. "I always wished someone would sing me a *serenata*. Young people nowadays know nothing about romance." She frowned. "They send a beep on your phone and that's it, you're engaged."

Alexis laughed. "Abuelita, it's not like that."

"Ah no?" Alpha shot her a challenging look. "Look at your cousin. Have you ever seen him bring a girl flowers or write a letter? He just beep beep on the phone and the girl beep back and that's it."

"She's right," Trini agreed. "In the old days, men were men and they treated women like precious flowers. That's how your granddaddy Lil Rafa won my heart." Trini sighed, resting her manicured palm over her heart. "The *serenata* is powerful. It can turn any frog into a prince." Trini caught herself. "Not that you're a frog, honey."

"Don't you two have anything better to do than put crazy ideas in Alexis's head?" Everyone turned at the severe tone in Fabi's voice.

Alexis glanced at her sister's frown. Fabi's stance was like a brick wall. The last time Fabi listened to Grandma Trini, she ended up dancing at her quinceañera with a handsome stranger who everyone swore was the devil. But this was different, she told herself. The *serenata* idea wasn't *that* crazy. It was just a little old-fashioned. Alexis glanced at Nikki.

"Alexis, it's perfect," Nikki said, her eyes growing bright. "Christian seems like the kind of guy who's big on theatrics. He does call himself El Charro Negro. I think he'd be blown away by a *serenata.* We can even get some people from the group to perform and everything."

"You think they would help?"

Nikki nodded. Alexis felt the excitement building in her stomach. The *serenata* was a pretty good idea. Christian would have to like it, she thought. He obviously liked mariachi — and who could resist a romantic gesture like this?

The following week, Alexis arrived late to mariachi rehearsal. The printer in the school library had run out of ink and she had to wait for the librarian to put in a new cartridge so she could finish printing her *serenata* lyrics. All weekend, she'd been searching for Spanish ballads without much luck. Most of the songs were about heartbreak or eternal love. Alexis needed something fun — like her. The librarian recommended the song "Me Gustas Mucho" — "I Like You a Lot." It was a cute, flirty song about a girl who didn't care what people said or how long it took, she would not give up or let anything come between them.

"Mr. Castillo?" Alexis asked.

"Assistant Principal Castillo," he corrected.

"Yes, I'm sorry, sir. I think we should try this song today," she said, smiling brightly.

AP Castillo reviewed the music. Overall, he was very supportive and encouraged Alexis to take an active part in leading the group — especially since everyone had started showing up on time for rehearsals after her unauthorized "field trip." Alexis played a version of the song sung by a legendary Mexican singer for the group on the CD player. No one seemed impressed. Then she told them about her plan to serenade Christian. That did the trick. Nikki, Marisol, and Karina thought it was romantic. The twins didn't believe she'd go through with it. Justin turned bright red, and Santiago fell out of his chair laughing. *He can stay home*, she thought.

Alexis was determined to whip the group into shape for her *serenata*. She forced herself to stay positive. All they needed was practice — lots of practice. She did not include her cousin in this analysis. Alexis winced as Santiago punched a bunch of random buttons on the accordion. She brought her hands to her ears. "What is that?" she asked, interrupting their practice. The group had been rehearsing the song all week. Alexis hoped that they would be ready to do the *serenata* by next Friday. But the new musicians were still learning their finger positioning, and Santiago . . . was doing his own thing.

"You like it, huh?" He smiled. "I've been trying to think of a way to make my sound special. I've been watching these videos with this guy named Steve Jordan. Man plays with his eyes closed and everything. He's the best, even bigger than Grandpa. I'm going to be like him."

"That's fine, but we're supposed to be playing together," Alexis reminded him, trying to make her voice sound calm. Time was slipping by, and soon Christian's group would be traveling across the state for competitions.

"Yo, *prima*, you can't rush art. Besides, I think it's better to be organic. Forget the music. Let's just play from our hearts." He threw the music sheets in the air with a dramatic flourish.

The rest of the group laughed until AP Castillo growled at Santiago to pick up his music and begin again. Castillo gave Santiago too many chances, Alexis thought. Her cousin never took anything seriously. Her heart dropped, and tears threatened to spill, as the musicians started to play her song. They were a mess. The guitars were off tempo. Karina kept complaining about her nails. But there was no going back, she told herself. The group had to get better. If she was ever going to get the chance to compete or get Christian to notice her, she had to get the group ready to perform. They were going to do the *serenata*, whether they were ready or not.

The day of the *serenata*, Alexis ate two plates of enchiladas with rice and beans. She was ravenous and scared out of her mind. She wanted to tell her grandmas about the *serenata*. But she was afraid of what they would do if Christian didn't appreciate her song. They were likely to go up to his apartment and drag him out by his hair. Alexis couldn't have that. She would have to do this *serenata* on her own.

As the mariachi members suited up in last year's outfits for the first time, AP Castillo lit up. The slightly used navy-blue uniforms, with shiny silver buttons and red sashes, transformed the rowdy high school bunch into a professional mariachi ensemble. Even Marisol looked the part, with her hair combed back in a clip. *She has the prettiest brown eyes*, Alexis thought, *when you can actually see them*.

However, nothing could disguise their sound. They weren't too bad for a group that had just started a couple of weeks ago, especially since many of the new members had never even held an instrument before. But they still weren't quite ready for a performance and especially not ready to serenade the regional champ. They were either really gutsy or clinically insane.

Luckily, Santiago had a backup plan for Alexis.

"Hey," he said, pulling Alexis off to the side. "I know you want to make a good impression on Mariachi Boy. But I think we still kind of suck." He smirked. "So I made this CD with your song and I thought we could just pretend to play behind you while you do the singing."

Alexis threw her arms around Santiago and pulled him into a hug. "Oh, Santi, you're the best." As she released him, she wondered, "Do you think the other guys will mind?"

Santiago laughed. "I think they'll be relieved. I saw Karina freaking out behind the Dumpster a minute ago."

The group got to Christian's apartment in the early evening. Shortly after their arrival, they saw Christian get home from his practice and go inside. Now Alexis and her bandmates were clustered on the sidewalk outside his building.

A couple of local boys leaned against a car hood, cracking jokes about them. Alexis ignored the boys and glanced at her group. Her friends looked good. She hoped she looked just as good. Alexis touched her hair to make sure the rose was in place. She'd borrowed her grandma Trini's big hoop earrings and dabbed some bacon grease behind her ears for luck. It was time. Alexis turned and gave Santiago a gesture to start the music.

Violin and trumpet sounds erupted into the night. Marisol did a stellar acting job pretending to play the violin. Then the twins and Nikki wiggled their fingers on their guitar strings along with the music. She waited for her cue and then, after taking a deep breath, Alexis opened her mouth.

She looked up at Christian's window and sang as she did a little dance in place. The boys on the car hood started to clap along with the beat. She was putting herself out there and Christian could totally reject her, but like Justin had said, mariachi made you feel bold and courageous. She knew she wouldn't regret doing this, no matter what the outcome was.

Lights started to flick on throughout the apartment complex. It reminded her of a big Christmas tree. Each apartment was lit except for his. Was he asleep? Alexis shook her worries off and continued to sing. Then the song came to an end. Her friends looked at her, wondering what to do next. His neighbors had come out to *oooh* and *aaah* at their outfits, but there was no sign of Christian. *No*, she thought, as her cheeks flared hot. *It can't end like this*. Alexis motioned to Santiago to replay the song. Maybe Christian hadn't heard them the first time?

Alexis got ready to sing as the music started again. She tried to calm her raging nerves. All of a sudden there was a hiccup and the song skipped, repeating the first notes over and over again. Alexis signaled for Santiago to turn it off, waving her arms frantically in the air. She glanced over her shoulder, praying that Christian wouldn't choose this moment to appear. This was more embarrassing than if she'd sung off-key. The music finally cut off. The deafening silence that followed created a huge lump of emotions at the back of her throat. Then the quiet night air was filled with howls of laughter. Alexis glared at the neighbors who'd come out to watch.

Alexis sighed. *This was a huge mistake.* Tears blurred her vision. She turned to march back to the car, but Nikki grabbed her arm. Alexis tried to shake her off, but Nikki swung her around and pointed up toward the apartments. Alexis didn't know what she was looking at until she heard the plucking of guitar chords. The tones wove together, producing a heart-melting melody.

Then a figure came out onto Christian's

balcony, singing and playing a guitar. Alexis felt her knees go weak. She didn't recognize the song, but it was lovely.

Suddenly, Christian disappeared from the balcony. Was he coming downstairs? Her heart leapt. This was actually happening! What would she say? She should have asked her grandmothers what to do after the *serenata*.

Alexis's train of thought died abruptly as Christian appeared in the driveway. He was repeating the chorus. She tried to look calm and collected — like she serenaded guys all the time. But Christian's presence scrambled her brain. He was now just a couple of feet away from her. He smiled as he lingered on the last note. It soared high above them like a dove flying in the sky. *Aaah! Now what?* The hairs on the back of Alexis's neck were standing on end. She wanted to say something, but her mouth didn't seem to work anymore. Christian looked at her expectantly.

"That was great," she finally said, in a breathless voice.

He smiled. "You weren't so bad yourself." He began to chuckle. "I especially like the guy who played the truck CD player. He's going places."

Alexis blushed.

Suddenly, a woman started yelling in Spanish really loudly. She called for Christian to come back inside. Alexis wondered who it was, but before she could ask, Christian pulled her away from the angry voice and down the street.

chapter 7

Alexis's mind whirled. A moment ago, she was serenading Christian. Now she was running behind him down the darkened streets of Mission. Christian glanced back at her and smiled. The gleam in his eye made her want to melt. He hadn't let go of her hand.

"Where are we going?" she stammered.

Christian laughed. "Not far, don't worry. I just wanted to talk to you away from our audience."

Alexis was thankful for the cover of darkness that concealed her hot cheeks.

"Hungry?" he asked, stopping in front of a pizza shop.

The bright, noisy fast-food restaurant jarred her senses. But then she smelled the food. "Starving," Alexis replied. "I'll have two slices of the Meat-Lovers' Delight with everything on it."

Christian smiled. "I think I will, too."

Alexis couldn't help but crack a smile. While he was ordering, Alexis sent a quick text to Santiago, so he wouldn't worry.

They grabbed their drinks and headed to an empty booth by the window. Christian stared at her expectantly. All of a sudden Alexis felt her nerves explode and her face start to sweat. *I'm sitting in a booth with Christian Luna!* She couldn't think of a word to say.

"That was some great singing back there," Christian finally said, leaning back in his plastic seat. Alexis did a double take. *Was that a compliment or a joke?* she wondered. He noticed her confused expression and started to turn bright red. "I mean, I thought it was cool. I never knew people actually did that sort of thing nowadays, you know?"

She took a big gulp from her drink. "Yeah, it was pretty crazy."

Christian stared at her from across the table as if she were some fascinating new species he'd just discovered. Then he leaned across the table and asked: "So why did you do it? You hardly know me. We met once, at the college day, right? How did you know I'd come out of my house?"

Just then the pizza arrived. Alexis reached for her slice and scarfed the piping-hot food down, burning the roof of her mouth. "I don't really know why I did it," she said between bites. "I just thought we should get to know each other. I'm a singer; you're a singer." She cringed at her words. They sounded lame, even to her ears.

Christian smiled. "You could have just come up to me, you know?"

"Yeah, but I'm sure lots of girls like you." Alexis blushed, but she couldn't stop herself. "I wanted to do something memorable. There's something about performing mariachi music that makes everything seem more vibrant and alive. When I heard you sing onstage, it made me want to sing back." Alexis covered her mouth with her hands. She'd said too much. Now she definitely sounded like an insane person.

Christian laughed in a friendly way. Alexis sighed with relief. "You are definitely something else," he said, chewing on his slice. "I think maybe you've been watching too many old movies. But I know what you mean about mariachi music making you feel alive. When I'm onstage I'm like this totally different person." He chuckled. "I like to wear all black, and pretend to be all deep, like some kind of rock star, but it's just an act."

"I don't think it's all an act," Alexis said softly. She thought back to Christian's words. "I think mariachi shows us our potential. Who we can become if we believe in ourselves and work hard."

Christian tilted his head at her. "Is that the speech you gave to the amateurs who pretended to play behind you tonight?"

She jerked back and shot him a hurt look.

"I'm sorry," he stammered, shaking his head. "Sometimes I don't think before I speak. What your friends did tonight was sweet. And I think they did a good job acting out their parts to the music."

"They may be amateurs, but they have heart. They've come a long way. You should have seen Santiago when he started. He didn't know how to hold an accordion upright at first, and Karina didn't even know what a harp was." Alexis was a little surprised to find herself defending her group members so fiercely. "They wanted to help me do this, but they weren't quite ready, so they offered to use the CD."

"I'm sorry I said anything about them. Really. I think it's great that they're learning music." His cheeks reddened and he turned to gaze out the front window. "I keep shoving my foot in my mouth." Then he looked back at Alexis and gave her a shy smile. "I guess you make me kind of nervous."

Alexis gasped. "Me? Make *you* nervous?"

Christian laughed, relaxing a bit. "Yeah, you. I don't think I've met anyone like you."

Alexis couldn't stop smiling.

Christian reached for Alexis's hand. His touch sent a jolt through her body. She looked up into his warm brown eyes.

He grinned back sheepishly and there was a pause. He took his hand away from hers and sipped his soda.

"Maybe I can do something to help your mariachi group."

"What?" Alexis was stunned. "You would help us?"

Christian shrugged. "Sure. It's the least I could do."

He wasn't a jerk, Alexis thought. *He wants to help our mariachi group!* Just then her phone vibrated. It was Santiago. When she gave him the address, he said he was coming to pick her up. Her heart dropped a bit; she didn't want this wonderful evening to end.

As they gathered up their trash, Alexis asked about the woman who had been yelling outside the apartment building.

"That was my mom." Christian winced.

Alexis shook herself. "We ran away from your mother?"

Christian rolled his eyes. "She's real strict. She wouldn't let me come down or even turn on the lights. I felt horrible when your song ended and I couldn't come out."

Alexis couldn't believe her ears. What was wrong with her? Didn't everyone like *serenatas*?

"You see," Christian explained, "my mom raised me all by herself. We left Mexico when I was still a baby. I never knew my dad. My mom worked three jobs and made sure I had the best music teachers. She used to sing in a pop band back in the eighties. They were called Radio

Bon Bon. But when she got pregnant, she had to give up her career. She's really protective." He smiled. "My mom is always on me about music first and stuff."

"That's the saddest story I've ever heard," Alexis said. "I can't imagine having to give up my dreams."

Christian nodded. "Yeah, I know. I owe her a lot. So I try really hard to make her proud. I want to show her that her hard work wasn't for nothing."

Alexis beamed. "You're a good son."

Christian's cheeks reddened. "Yeah, I just have no life. School. Mariachi. Homework. Bed." He shrugged. "That's all I do."

"Ha!" Alexis laughed, rolling her eyes. "I don't feel sorry for you, Mr. Regional Champ."

He smiled playfully. "Winning that was pretty cool."

A car honked out front. It was Santiago, waving from his truck. Alexis and Christian got up at the same time.

"That's for me," Alexis said, letting out a sigh. She felt cheated. Here he was, her destiny in the flesh, and she had to go home. They stood in front of each other, toe-to-toe. She bit her lower lip. "So I guess your mom doesn't let you see much of your friends, or you know, go on dates."

Christian smiled. He was so cute, he made her feel woozy. "Well, that's technically true. I'm not really supposed to date . . . but there are exceptions."

She gave him a curious look. "Exceptions?" Alexis wondered, feeling her pulse quicken.

He smiled. "And since you happen to be pretty exceptional . . ."

"Really?"

Christian shrugged. "Absolutely. This is my life. My mom gave up a lot for me, but that doesn't mean I have to do everything her way."

Alexis wanted to scream, but she tried to play it cool. "So, I guess I'll see you around soon?"

"Definitely," he said, blushing hard.

Alexis attempted to give him a quick hug just as Christian tried to hug her. Their arms tangled, foreheads bumped, and lips met. Alexis froze in disbelief. Were they actually kissing? Neither one moved. Then the sound of Santiago's honk jerked them free. That was not exactly how she'd pictured their first kiss going. She raised her fingers to her lips in surprise. But still, it had been nice. The memory of the pressure of his lips left her light-headed. Santiago honked again.

"I have to go," Alexis said, hurrying out of the pizzeria.

When Santiago dropped her off, Alexis found her bedroom crowded with guests. Her sister perched on the windowsill with her grandma Trini. On her twin bed sat her mom and dad and baby brother. Across from them sat her abuelita Alpha and grandpa Frank. All that was missing was Chuy the cook, she thought.

Alexis stretched her arms above her head

[107]

and yawned. "Wow, am I tired. I had a really long day. . . ." she began, ignoring the desperate looks from her family. "Fabi, will you get the light on your way out?"

"We know you did the *serenata* tonight!" Trini cried, throwing her arms up.

Her mother bounced with excitement. "So, how was it? Did he like it?"

"Did you sing 'Cielito Lindo'?" Alpha asked. "I love that song."

"No, 'Por un Amor,' now that's a real song," Grandpa Frank interrupted, slapping his gums. He must have come in a hurry, because he'd forgotten to put in his dentures.

Alexis looked at the faces staring at her. Their eyes beamed with excitement. *What a bunch of hopeless romantics*, she thought. She sighed, giving in to the pressure, and took a seat between her mom and dad on her pink comforter.

"Well, at first I didn't think he would show. . . ." Alexis told them the whole story.

They listened, captivated, like she was a heroine in her own soap opera. She left out the part about his mother screaming after them and not wanting him to date and skipped to their accidental kiss. The group cheered.

That Monday, Alexis couldn't wait for school to end so she could see her bandmates. Her friends must have been dying with curiosity, she thought, when she took off after the *serenata*. Nikki already knew all the details. But Alexis didn't have Karina's or Marisol's numbers, so she had to wait until rehearsal to tell them the story. She also wanted to tell the group about Christian's offer of help. With his expert support, the group was sure to improve.

She bumped into AP Castillo on the stairs. He was cursing under his breath and wasn't watching where he was going.

"Are you coming to practice?" Alexis asked.

"I don't know what to do anymore. Those guys are such a bunch of clowns." He motioned toward the practice room with frustration. "I thought I could help. I really believed that music would turn them around. The principal is breathing down my neck. He thinks I'm wasting my time. He wants to get rid of the class."

"Please, don't go," Alexis said. "Let me talk to them, please."

"And your cousin is nowhere to be found." He grunted. "I can't talk right now. I'm really ticked off."

Confused, Alexis ran the rest of the way to the rehearsal space. The room was in chaos. Hip-hop beats were bumping from the CD player. A few guys were twirling around the middle of the floor, trying to make themselves dizzy. The twins were drawing all over the whiteboard. Alexis was relieved when she noticed they were just using dry-erase markers. Karina was screaming into her phone at someone, and Marisol was in a corner reading. Nikki and Justin stared, wide-eyed, from the opposite side of the room. They were clutching their instruments to their chests like life preservers.

Alexis marched over to the CD player and turned it off. Gripes and groans erupted from the dancers. "What did you guys say to Castillo?" Alexis cried.

Pablo scratched his bald head. "Oh, we gave Castillo the day off. We're celebrating, can't you see? Santi told us about your date, so we thought we deserved a little R & R." He moved to turn the music back on, but Alexis blocked his path.

"You think this is all some kind of joke?"

He frowned. "What do you mean?"

"Castillo. Mariachi class. You know the principal wants to cut the program."

Pablo shrugged. "So, why is that my problem? I didn't ask for his help. I don't get why you're so mad. You got the boy. Now we're celebrating. It's a happy ending for everyone."

"You don't get it." Alexis groaned, raising her arms in the air. Then she noticed that everyone was looking at her as if she were possessed.

The *serenata* had backfired. It was a success in some ways. She had gotten Christian's attention — and his number! But it was a flop for the ensemble. They hadn't actually played a successful song. Looking around the room, it seemed like everyone had lost interest in the music. She remembered her conversation with Christian. How she'd defended her bandmates and how mariachi music was so full of passion and soul, but the people who needed to feel that the most were right here in this room. Alexis realized that she'd failed her group. In her single-minded attempt to woo Christian, she'd totally forgotten what was most important in all of this — the music.

Alexis had used her bandmates to make her look good. And they went along with it, not because they believed in the power of the music or the team, but because they liked her. Tears blurred her eyes.

"Whoa, whoa," Pablo said, putting his arm around her. "I didn't mean to make you cry. I just thought we could hang out a little, you know, chill out."

"It's not that." She shook her head, wiping her nose on her sleeve. "I feel horrible. I've been just thinking about my career goals and trying to impress Christian and I forgot what mariachi was really about."

"I liked doing the *serenata*," Nikki said in a quiet voice behind her.

"Me, too," Karina added, snapping her phone closed. "Even though we didn't really play, I looked good in my *charro* outfit. Did you see how the people looked at us?" She beamed and clapped her hands. "It was sweet."

"Yo," Pedro cut in. "You should've seen the look on our mom's face when we got home. I've only seen my moms cry once before, when my pops got out of jail. It felt real nice to see her smile like that." His brother, Pablo, nodded in agreement.

Alexis was shocked. "So you don't think I'm a selfish, self-absorbed *fresa*?"

"Maybe not selfish," Karina said with a smirk. "But definitely a *fresa*."

Alexis laughed. This mariachi ensemble was nothing like she'd expected it to be. She beamed at the group. "Oh, wait, but what about Castillo? I've never seen him so mad before. I think he quit."

"You don't have to worry about me," a voice called from the doorway. "I'm no quitter." AP Castillo pushed someone in front of him. It was Santiago, smiling brightly as if nothing was wrong. AP Castillo followed after him, eyeing Santiago like a hawk. Castillo glanced around the room and frowned at the sight. "I see everyone is here now. I've got some news for you guys." He paused to make sure everyone was listening. "You guys got yourself a real competition," he announced.

"You can't do this," Alexis cried. "We're not ready yet."

AP Castillo smiled. "Oh, yes I can. Don't worry. It's not a traditional competition, and it won't be against any of the schools here in the Valley. I just got off the phone with a friend of mine who teaches near Dallas. They're having a chilifest and a couple of the newer school mariachi clubs are going to have a friendly competition. I think it will be good for you guys."

"Can't we just watch from the audience?" Santiago asked.

"Nope," Castillo stated, crossing his arms. "Besides, I already said we'd be there."

"When's the festival?" Alexis asked.

"In three weeks."

chapter 8

I hate this damn thing," Karina cried out in frustration in the middle of rehearsal the following week. "Look, I broke another nail." She fanned her fingers in the air.

"Ayyy, poor baby," Pablo said in a pouty baby voice behind her.

"I heard that," Karina snapped.

"Okay, guys." Justin rose from his seat. His big brown eyes were full of warmth and understanding. "I know we're all worried about the performance coming up, but we can't turn on each other. We're a team."

"That's right," AP Castillo said. "There's nothing to be worried about. But, Karina, I can tell you haven't been practicing."

"Well, maybe I'm just too stupid for this instrument," she said, hitting the harp in frustration.

Alexis was about to jump in when a familiar voice interrupted. "Her hands are all wrong."

The whole class turned. Christian Luna smiled from the doorway. He looked like a ray of golden sunshine in the dreary gray room. Christian locked eyes with Alexis. Her heart leapt. Christian's busy practice schedule had kept them apart since the *serenata*, but finally, here he was. Alexis tried to stay calm, but she couldn't keep herself from grinning.

"Your hand is all wrong," Christian continued in a kind voice. "Look, your right hand needs to be relaxed and curved — like you're holding a baby chick." He adjusted Karina's right elbow so it gave her easier mobility. "And your left elbow should be out, in an L shape."

He pulled her left arm into position. "Like that. Now try playing a C chord."

Karina looked confused.

"The red chord," Christian prompted. He caught Alexis's eye over his shoulder as Karina plucked the chord. The sound was crisp and clear and her nails remained intact.

Castillo cleared his throat. "Thank you, young man. You seem to know a lot about music. Want a job?"

Christian laughed. "Thank you, but I already have a lot on my plate. I just stopped by today because Alexis said you guys might need a little help."

The guitarists, *guitarrón*, and *vihuela* players circled around Christian. He led them in a series of exercises. The musicians took to him like he was one of the team. Alexis caught him looking in her direction as he strummed the chords on the *vihuela* at a slow pace so that the others could follow. Christian's eyes sparkled as he encouraged the struggling twins to keep up. At the end of rehearsal, everyone was smiling. The group was far from ready to compete, but they were getting better.

After practice, Christian invited Alexis out to dinner. Alexis called her mom for permission to stay out late and to tell her all about Christian's surprise visit. Magda told her to have fun and promised to wait up to get all the details. Christian took Alexis to a fancy restaurant in La Joya that had a thatched roof woven with palm-tree leaves. They sat on the patio, which overlooked a large pond. It felt like a dream to be sitting with Christian, sipping on virgin margaritas. Glancing at the menu, she noticed how expensive all the dishes were. The fajitas were twice what her parents charged at their restaurant.

A band started to play. The musicians approached the line of tables, taking requests for a small fee. They played "Solamente una Vez." Alexis couldn't help singing softly with them as she sipped from her glass and swayed to the chorus.

"Do you want to sing?" Christian asked.

Alexis shook her head. "Not now. I just like listening."

His eyes sparkled as he reached to hold her hand. "What other mariachi songs do you like?"

Alexis took another sip from her drink and smiled. "Well, I actually have a confession to make. I just started learning mariachi songs last year."

"Really?"

"I know all the famous songs everyone knows, like 'Volver Volver' and 'El Rey,' and of course 'Las Mañanitas.' But I didn't really get into it until recently. I grew up singing my grandpa's *conjunto* music. *Puro Tex-Mex*," she said, imitating her grandma Trini.

"Aah, I get it. So music runs in your family."

"Yeah, I guess. My grandfather was really famous in his time. He's even in the Tejano

Roots Hall of Fame museum. It's a small picture by the water fountain, but he's there."

Christian smiled, looking impressed.

Alexis licked her lips. "One day, I'll be there, too — at least, I hope so." She felt her cheeks get hot. "What about you? What kind of music do you like?"

He shrugged. "I like all kinds of music. Recently I've even started writing my own *rancheras*."

"Really?" Alexis couldn't hide her interest. "What do you write about?"

Christian's cheeks reddened. "Promise not to laugh?" Alexis nodded. "Well, I wrote this one song about these two brothers who were wanted for breaking hearts and breaking heads on both sides of the Rio Grande." He laughed. "It's so corny." Christian sang the last line out loud. "If you see the Salinas brothers coming near your daughter/Let them steal a kiss, if you value your heart." He smiled proudly when he was done.

Alexis jerked like she'd been rudely awakened from a beautiful dream. "Wait! Are you talking about Brandon and Travis Salinas?"

"You know them?" Christian asked.

Alexis thought about the song in Karina's truck and the way Christian had looked so familiar to her at the university concert. He didn't just remind her of the guy she'd seen with the Salinas brothers — he was that guy. The Salinas brothers were always getting her cousin into trouble. "Those knuckleheads would get slapped all the way to Hidalgo if they tried to steal a kiss from me," she said.

Christian laughed. "I bet they would!" Then he took a deep breath and said: "That's just what they wanted me to sing for them, though. I didn't make up the words. I just arranged the lyrics with the music so they sounded good."

"So they paid you to write songs about them?"

Christian nodded. "Yeah. I've done it for other people, too. For two hundred bucks I'll even sing it and make them a CD."

It was suddenly clear to Alexis how Christian could afford to treat her to such a nice dinner. She wasn't sure she liked knowing he took money from people like the Salinas brothers.

"Isn't that lying? Brandon and Travis didn't shoot up a town."

"It's just fiction." He gestured like it was no big deal. "Like in the movies."

Alexis pressed her lips together. This was definitely different than some old movie. "It sounds a lot like you're writing *narcocorridos*."

Christian sat up straight. "I wish. Those guys make thousands of dollars for songs." He noticed Alexis's disapproval and lowered his voice. "I probably wouldn't do it if I didn't really need the money. I'm trying to save up for college, you know? I'm not a citizen. The out-of-state tuition is steep. That's why I've been working so hard, and writing these songs on the side."

Alexis softened. "It's not fair," she whispered, growing upset.

Christian smiled. "The University of Texas has the best music program in the country. They have this scholarship —"

"Oh, I'm sure you'll get it. You're the best," Alexis interrupted. She frowned at the checkered tablecloth on the table. She couldn't get his songwriting out of her head. "Writing *narcocorridos* is dangerous. What if the Salinas brothers don't like your song? People get killed over those songs. My grandma Alpha says they're illegal to play on the radio in Mexico."

The roving musicians approached their table and asked if they wanted a song, just as the sizzling fajitas arrived. Christian nodded for her to pick one. When she wouldn't, he leaned over to the guitar player and asked for a song.

The musicians plucked expertly at their instruments, producing a quick *chachacha* beat. She had heard the song before. But when Christian began to sing the lyrics to her, she thought she was going to melt. He sang about dark eyes, cinnamon skin, and colorful flowers. It didn't matter that the song wasn't written for her. Alexis wanted to pretend that it was. She waited for the chorus to come around and sang back:

"Me importas tú, y tú, y tú, y solamente tú."

It was the perfect song to declare that they liked each other. The couples seated around them turned with bright eyes and dancing smiles. Christian rose from his chair. He took Alexis's hand, lifting her up and spinning her slowly with the beat of the music. When the song ended, the crowd cheered. Alexis blushed. She hadn't realized they were making such a scene. But she was too happy to be embarrassed.

Suddenly, a familiar cackling voice shouted for another one. Alexis looked to see where the request came from and stopped when she spotted a shadowy figure seated all alone at the far end of the establishment. Was that the old woman from the *botánica*? *"La bruja!"* She gasped in disbelief.

The musicians nodded and began to play the traditional Veracruz classic. Christian shot Alexis a confused look. She waved him away and told him that she had to go to the bathroom. Alexis's heart pounded as she made her way toward the woman from the *botánica*. What was she doing here? It seemed too strange to be just a coincidence. The old woman couldn't have any idea that Alexis had found the boy she'd been longing for, could she?

When she reached the table she thought the woman had been seated at, no one was there. Alexis looked around, shaking her head in confusion.

A cool wind swept past her, making the hairs on her arms stand on end. She rubbed her arms and peered out into the darkness. Bright yellow eyes blinked back from a nearby tree.

Suddenly, Christian called out to her. Alexis turned, relieved at the interruption. She started to walk toward him when she heard an owl cry. Her heart thumped as she thought about the *Lechuza* stories she'd heard as a child. *Old women who turn into owls don't really exist — right?* Alexis reassured herself. She slowly glanced over her shoulder, back to where she'd seen the yellow eyes. But there was nothing there. Had she imagined it?

Alexis refused to allow the spooky moment at the restaurant to darken her weekend. Her date with Christian had been too good to be true. Alexis was so happy, she wanted the whole world to celebrate with her. A fun polka was playing on the jukebox at her family's restaurant when she walked in. Alexis bobbed her head in time with the beat. She kissed her grandpa Frank on his warm cheek, almost making him spill his coffee. When she tried to twirl her sister, Fabi, around like they were on a dance floor, her sister cried: "What's gotten into you?"

Alexis sighed. "I just love life."

Her sister rolled her eyes and handed her a bucket. "All right, Twinkle Toes, then why don't you show that table some love and clear it." She gestured toward the front of the room.

"No problem," Alexis replied, swaying her hips across the floor. "I love to help." She hummed along to the music as she set several dirtied plates, cups, and crumpled napkins into the bucket.

The door chimed behind her, but Alexis hardly noticed. Her head was filled with blissful memories of the night before. She pressed her fingertips lightly to her mouth. Christian's sweet lips had left a permanent imprint. She couldn't wait to kiss him again.

"Are you Alexis Garza?" a voice behind her asked.

"That's me. Can I help you with something?" Alexis asked.

A woman loomed in front of her. She had thick, hairy arms covered in gold bracelets and wore a flashy floral-print dress. She had a handsome face, but her eyes were so severe that Alexis felt like they were trying to stab her. "I am Viola Luna, Christian's mamá," she said in a thick Spanish accent.

Alexis jolted. Christian's stories about his mom being strict and controlling had made her feel anxious about meeting her. *But she's here at the restaurant now*, Alexis thought. *Maybe she's come to say hello and reach out to Christian's new girlfriend?* Alexis's smile brightened in anticipation. She wiped her hands on her jeans and started to introduce herself.

Viola looked at her hand and frowned. "Christian has no time for girls. He needs to practice." Although Mrs. Luna's words were harsh, her eyes gave away her deep concern. "He has a big audition for college soon."

"Oh, I had no idea."

"Christian is always gone. He says he's studying, but he doesn't take his instruments. Stay away from my Christian. He's my only son. I don't want him to lose this chance we've worked so hard for."

chapter 9

Alexis stared as the door chimed closed behind Viola Luna. Her first thought was to call Christian and tell him about her encounter with his mother. But then she thought about his upcoming audition and his need to stay focused. She didn't want to jeopardize anything for him.

"You all right?" her sister asked, startling Alexis with her cold touch.

"I'm fine," Alexis said after a moment. "That was Christian's mom. She told me to stay away from her son."

"Really?"

"Yeah, like I'm some kind of bad influence. Can you believe it?"

Their mother walked up to them. She put her hands on her hips in a no-nonsense manner. Despite her mother's petite size, she commanded order with her sheer presence. "There're customers waiting to sit." She motioned toward a group of four standing by the door. *"Muévanse,"* she ordered.

Fabi jumped and grabbed a couple of forks from the table and tossed them into the dish bucket. Alexis wiped the table clean as her sister prepared it for the next customers. Then she carried the heavy bucket and her heavy heart back to the kitchen.

Christian called her several times over the weekend. Alexis texted him that she was sick, *probably contagious, actually.* Alexis didn't want to lie, but the truth was so much harder. Christian had a blossoming career to think about, and she didn't want to get in the way. She would keep away until his audition, she told herself. After that, she wouldn't let anyone keep them apart. The thought of his mother made her break out in a nervous sweat. She quickly removed the image of Viola Luna's angry frown from her mind.

Instead, she thought about the mariachi ensemble. Since Christian's visit last week, the group seemed more focused and driven. Their first performance was coming up fast.

Maybe it won't be so bad, she told herself, trying to put on a smile as she arrived to practice the following school day. At least the group looked good in their *charro* outfits.

As she opened the door, the sounds of people shouting alarmed her. Her bandmates were yelling and pointing fingers at one another. Pedro pushed Justin against the wall while AP Castillo yelled at Santiago. Karina threatened Pablo with her fists in the air, and Nikki was bawling her eyes out in a chair.

"What is going on here?" Alexis gasped.

"He did it," Karina said, pointing at Pablo.

"I didn't do nothing, you freak," Pablo spat back.

"You've really done it this time," AP Castillo said in a threatening manner to Santiago. "No more second chances for you."

Santiago raised his arm as if to block a blow. "I didn't touch them. I swear."

"Touch what?" Alexis asked. "Will someone tell me what's going on?"

Nikki looked up with tearful eyes. Her voice shook as she spoke: "Someone stole the maria-chi *trajes*."

"What?"

"They took everything," Nikki cried. Tears spilled down her cheeks. Alexis felt like she'd been punched in the stomach. Nikki wiped her nose on her sleeve and peered up at Alexis. "I came early to Febreze them and air them out." She held up a little spray bottle. "But when I got here, I noticed the locker had been broken into and all our outfits were gone. They took everything." She sniffed. "They even took the pita-style belts my dad bought in Tampico."

Karina reached for Pablo. "I know you know who took them."

Pablo jumped out of her reach. "You're crazy. You think I would let one of my boys steal from me? That was my *traje*, too, you know."

Karina threw her fists in the air. "Well, somebody took them." The group hurled accusations and insults across the room like daggers.

"Please stop," Alexis cried over the noise. "This isn't fixing anything." The shouting stopped. Alexis sighed with relief. "Look, let's think about what we're going to do."

"Why don't we go look for them," Marisol suggested in a quiet voice. Everyone turned to look at her, because she hardly ever spoke up in a large crowd. "Sometimes people steal things just for fun." She paused, turning bright red. "Maybe the *trajes* are just stuffed in a Dumpster or a trash can somewhere."

"Good thinking," Alexis said, flashing her a bright smile. "Why don't you and some of the others go have a look around the school and see if the uniforms got dumped somewhere?"

Marisol nodded. The twins stood to follow her out of the room.

"And what happens if we don't find them?" Pedro asked.

"Well ..." Alexis looked at AP Castillo for help.

He shook his head and sucked in through his teeth. "There's no mariachi fund, and the school is already facing major budget cuts. We're on our own."

"Yikes," Pedro muttered as he, Pablo, and Marisol tramped out of the room.

"We'll find the money, if we need to," Alexis said, trying to sound more confident than she felt.

"Do you even know how much outfits like those cost?" Karina asked in an exasperated tone.

She was not helping, Alexis thought.

AP Castillo sat down in one of the folding chairs. "You don't need the *trajes* to perform."

"Oh, hell no," Santiago cried. "The suits were the only thing good about us. You throw us out there in our street clothes, and we won't have anything going for us. People will laugh."

AP Castillo sighed deeply. Alexis noticed that his hair looked grayer than usual. She glanced at the other students. They looked deflated. *It's not fair*, Alexis thought. *We've worked so hard!*

"We have to at least try," Alexis pleaded. She pulled at Santiago's limp arm and walked over to Nikki. "We can do this. Let's start thinking of possible fund-raising activities. We're starting to sound like a real band now. I want to perform with you guys! Who's with me?"

There was silence. Alexis's heart dropped. Then she heard someone move on her right.

"I'm with you," Justin said, stepping forward. She gave him an appreciative smile.

"Me, too," Karina said from the back.

AP Castillo looked up at Alexis. "What do you say, AP Castillo?" Alexis asked.

The man cleared his throat, trying to bury his emotion. "I like your spunk, Garza. I'm with you."

Just then, the trio of searchers rushed into the practice room. Marisol held out a busted sombrero and a ripped jacket. Everyone stared sadly at her, their hopes for finding the uniforms dissolving before their eyes.

"Well," Alexis said, forcing a cheerful attitude, "fund-raising starts now, then!"

The bandmates put all their energy into holding bake sales, doing candygrams, and collecting cans. They even went door-to-door to ask for donations. It was hard getting money, but Alexis tried to keep everyone's enthusiasm up.

"C'mon, guys," Alexis said one afternoon, leading a couple members of the group to the HEB grocery store on Main Street. The manager was Nikki's cousin, and he had agreed to let them perform for tips inside. Shoppers stared at the group as they set up by the bakery. Alexis could tell that her friends were nervous. Most of them had never performed for an audience before — not counting the excellent pretend playing they'd done during her *serenata*. Karina kept looking at the ground, and Pablo and Pedro were pushing each other into shopping carts. "Settle down, guys," Alexis said, trying to calm their nerves. "Remember that we're trying to raise money for our uniforms."

"We'll be fine," Nikki agreed, holding her *guitarrón*. "Just do your best."

"Hello? We suck." Karina fidgeted from one foot to the other. "No one is going to give us money."

"Yes, they will," Alexis said, giving her a wink. "Watch." Alexis turned to the HEB customers: "Good afternoon, ladies and gentlemen. We are the Dos Rios mariachi group and we are raising money to buy mariachi uniforms. We would appreciate any support." She nodded to Nikki and the twins.

The three began playing the beginning melody to the song "Serenata Huasteca." Alexis gave Karina a nod. Karina smiled as Justin began to blow his trumpet. The group was getting better. A crowd began to form around them. Some people threw coins in their bucket. Alexis came in on cue and sang the sweet serenade. She made eye contact with the customers and even flirted with a shy three-year-old boy who hid behind his mother's skirt. After singing the first stanza, she accompanied Marisol on the violin. Marisol looked grateful. She was still struggling to keep up with the rest of the group.

Alexis had just put her instrument down to

sing the second stanza when a male voice jumped in. Alexis turned, shocked by the interruption. Her heart jumped when she recognized Christian leaning on a shopping cart. His mother stood at the end of the aisle with a grumpy expression on her face. Christian abandoned the shopping cart and came up to the group. He smiled as he continued to sing the song. Hearing his voice come to her rescue made Alexis light up with joy, and she realized how much she missed seeing him. Together they sang the chorus.

The music ended with a round of applause and customers passing the bucket around. Alexis couldn't believe that Christian was right here, in her town, shopping. She felt guilty that she'd been avoiding him, but happy to see him.

"What are you doing out here?" Alexis whispered.

"My mom needed to get some stuff for my *tía*, who lives out here near Los Gatos.

What are all you guys doing here singing mariachi songs?"

Alexis frowned. "Our *trajes* were stolen and we're trying to raise money to pay for new ones, before our first competition."

Christian's face dropped. "That's terrible. I can't believe someone would do that." He reached into his pocket and pulled out ten dollars. He put it in the bucket. "My contribution," he said, with a big grin.

"Christian," his mother called. She gestured to him sharply.

He glanced at his mom and back at Alexis. "I got to go," he whispered. "Call you later." Christian hurried to catch up with his mother.

Alexis watched him leave. She wished he could stay and sing more songs with the group. Then she heard someone in the audience request the song "Me Gustas Mucho." Alexis turned to the group. They smiled back at her, ready to play.

Later that week, Christian called Alexis as she walked home from the restaurant. Alexis had been so busy with fund-raising lately that she'd almost been able to not think about how much she wanted to see him, scary overprotective mom or not.

"Hey," Christian said. "Where have you been? I've been trying to reach you all week. You can't be singing at grocery stores all the time."

The sound of his voice made her heart leap. "I'm sorry." Alexis grinned. "The group has been going crazy trying to raise money. How are you?"

"Remember when I told you there was a scholarship I was trying to get? I didn't tell you the auditions were today, because I didn't know what my chances were and I didn't want to get my hopes up."

"Today?" Alexis exclaimed. Her whole body started to tingle with excitement.

"I think I did well. I won't know for sure for a couple weeks. But I just gave the best audition of my life. I think I have a good chance of getting the scholarship."

"Really? That's great!" Alexis cheered. A warm sensation filled her chest. Now that Christian had auditioned for his important scholarship, Alexis didn't have to worry that she was distracting him from his dreams. "We should celebrate. Let's go out tonight."

"Yeah, let's go do something fun."

Alexis puckered her lips. "I'll think of something."

She hung up just as a truck honked. Alexis glanced over her shoulder. It was Santiago. He pulled up alongside her. "Hey, you, hop in." He motioned, shaking his dark curls.

Alexis jumped in and put on her seat belt. They were only three blocks from her house, but her cousin had a lead foot. *Better safe than in the hospital with a broken rib*, she thought.

"Hey, so I had this idea," Santiago started. "You know how we're raising money for mariachi and everything." Alexis nodded for him to continue. "Well" — he paused and glanced over his shoulder as if he thought he was being followed — "I got a call a little while ago about a race tonight. I was going to tell the dude to shove it, but then I thought about the group and how we needed money, you know? I was thinking . . . if I win I could give all the money to the band." He glanced sideways at Alexis to gauge her reaction.

Alexis was so touched by his desire to be helpful that she ignored a small twinge of worry about him racing. She gave him a hug. "I think it's a great idea."

"You do?" Santiago relaxed. "Cool."

"Hey, maybe Christian and I can come along? You know, to give you support?"

Her cousin nodded. "I should say no, but who am I to turn down adoring fans?" He stopped in front of her house, braking so fast Alexis thought she might get whiplash. "I'll pick you guys up at ten."

When Santiago, Alexis, and Christian arrived at the race, festivities were already in full swing. A dozen car headlights lit up a central area where people were singing, dancing, and laughing into the night.

Santiago headed over to a couple of his buddies, who were in charge of the races. Alexis strolled arm in arm with Christian through the crowds. Suddenly, Christian stopped and tilted his head to listen to something. His eyes got bright and he led Alexis to a group of people singing a *ranchera*.

The group was hidden behind a cloud of smoke. In the center of the circle stood the Salinas brothers. She could tell they were drunk by the way they were hanging all over each other, singing loudly and really off-key.

When they recognized Christian, the brothers hooted.

"Yo," Brandon Salinas announced to the group. He put an arm around Christian and pulled him over to the music. "This is the guy I was telling you about. El Charro Negro."

Alexis looked around at the rest of the group. Her eyes stopped on a girl with red highlights, violet contacts, and a mean scowl.

"Karina! What are you doing here?"

Her bandmate was wearing a tiered gold-colored tube dress that looked out of place in the middle of the countryside. Karina looked up and her frown melted. "Hey — Alexis! I guess I'm babysitting tonight." She gestured at Brandon, who was falling all over Christian. Behind them, Alexis noticed his brother, Travis, talking to a bunch of mean-looking men behind the truck.

"I didn't know Brandon was the boyfriend you talked about," Alexis said.

Karina winced. "We're not exactly dating.

He calls me sometimes and we go out and party." She shrugged. "I don't even know why I'm still here. I thought . . . I thought he was going to take me out on a real date, you know?" She looked down at her dress. "I'm such a fool," she said, kicking the dirt.

"He's the fool," Alexis said, gesturing in Brandon's direction. He had fallen to the ground and three people were trying to get him back up. "You're too good for him."

Karina glanced sideways at her. "You're just saying that to make me feel better."

"Oh, come on," Alexis said. "You have a big heart and you're getting pretty good on the harp. You could have quit a long time ago, but you stuck with it and it shows. Brandon doesn't deserve you. You deserve to be with a guy who will take you out on real dates, say nice things to you, or even serenade you."

Karina smiled. "You're right." She looked at Brandon and sighed. "Let's ditch this group. C'mon."

Alexis turned to look back at Christian as Karina pulled her away. He motioned for her not to worry and he'd catch up.

The girls went to the starting line to get good spots. Santiago waved from his car as he prepared. When he took off, Alexis and Karina cheered until their chests hurt. Alexis watched as Santiago's red taillights blinked out in the night. She prayed that he would not hit any potholes or small animals.

"C'mon," Alexis said, grabbing Karina's hand. She led her through the crowd toward the finish line. As she snaked through the crowd, she kept an eye out for Christian. Where was he?

They waited nervously until the two trucks emerged around the bend at the same time. Alexis screamed. *It's too close*, she thought, biting her nails. The trucks reached the finish line at what seemed like the exact same time. The pressure from their engines picked up dirt and tossed it all around them, creating a dark cloud.

"Who won?" Alexis cried, jumping up and trying to see past a guy's cowboy hat.

"I can't see a thing," Karina said beside her.

Alexis pulled Karina through the standing bodies to the clearing. People were shouting and hooting. But she couldn't tell who'd won. Then she saw her cousin standing by his truck talking to one of the guys. The guy handed him a roll of bills.

"He won!" Alexis cried. She leapt into Karina's arms and the two jumped up and down with excitement. Alexis waved at her cousin, but he wasn't looking her way. Santiago was paying close attention to a guy next to him and she could tell by the scowl on his face that he didn't like what he was hearing.

Santiago looked up and caught Alexis's eye. He motioned for her to come over quickly. Alexis grabbed Karina by the hand and pushed her way through the spectators.

Suddenly, the place lit up with red and blue blinking lights. Alexis heard the familiar siren of a police car and felt her blood run cold.

"Oh, my God," Karina screamed in Alexis's ear. "It's *la chota*."

chapter 10

The crowd was trying to flee. Bodies bumped into her, pushing her back and forth like a palm tree in a hurricane. Alexis looked for Santiago or Christian, but she didn't recognize the faces around her. Fear gripped her heart. Voices screamed as motors roared to life. Alexis froze, paralyzed by the situation. She didn't know where to go.

Suddenly, a hand grabbed hers and pulled her through the crowd. She allowed herself to be dragged to the far end of the clearing and behind a yellow Ford truck. When they were a safe distance from the mob, she looked up and into the eyes of her cousin Santiago.

"We've got to get out of here," he said, sweating profusely.

Alexis's chest tightened with worry. "We have to find Karina and Christian. I won't leave them behind."

"I don't think we have a choice," Santiago said, gesturing to the wall of uniformed officers rounding people up.

"I can't leave them," Alexis cried, tears stinging her eyes. This was a horrible mess. *I never should have come here.*

"Don't be stupid," Santiago said, taking her by the wrist. "We have to get out of here — fast." He pulled her to his truck. Alexis looked for her friends amid the sea of faces. She had to find them.

Santiago pushed Alexis into his truck. She understood her cousin's apprehension. They'd be in huge trouble if they got caught. But that was nothing compared to what would happen to Christian. Drag races were illegal — and Christian didn't have papers! What would they do to him? Coming here tonight was her idea. Alexis bit down so hard on her lower lip that she drew blood. Her cousin started the engine, but he didn't turn on his headlights. He had just put the truck in drive when Alexis screamed.

"There's Karina! Right over there." Alexis pointed toward the mob.

"I ain't going back there," he said, shaking his head.

"Just wait a second." Alexis lowered the window and waved frantically, calling out to Karina.

She glanced toward Alexis and ran straight for the truck. Alexis threw open the door for Karina to jump in.

"Drive!" Karina screamed as she climbed into the seat.

Santiago pushed down on the pedal and the truck dashed out into the night. Alexis couldn't believe that they were leaving. She hoped Christian would be okay. She had left him talking to the Salinas brothers — surely they wouldn't let themselves get caught? Her heart swelled as her lungs constricted.

Beside her, Karina reached out for Alexis's hand and clutched it tightly. No one spoke as they drove. Alexis pressed her lips tightly together as they bounced and jerked through the wilderness in the moonless night.

She shouldn't have let Santiago race. Her gut had warned her against it. If only she'd listened to it. If only they hadn't needed the money so badly. This had seemed like such a simple way to replace the uniforms. *If only I hadn't invited Christian! If only we hadn't gotten separated!* Alexis squeezed her eyes shut and tried to push images of officers clubbing him with their batons or arresting him out of her mind.

He would get away, she told herself. He had to.

•　•　•

"*Mija*, what happened to your cell phone? I tried calling you all morning," her mother asked the next day at the family restaurant.

A shiver raced down Alexis's back. "I lost it," she mumbled into the hot chocolate she was drinking out of a clay mug. It must have fallen out of her back pocket, she thought. What if the cops found it? She swallowed hard. Alexis had tried calling Christian several times from her home phone, but his calls went straight to voice mail. She was sick with worry, but she couldn't tell anyone about it. Her mother would hit the roof if she found out where Alexis had been.

"You better cancel that phone right away," her grandmother Alpha called. She sat at the counter with the morning paper in her hands. "*La mafia* steals phones, you know. They do all their dirty negotiations and you get hit with the bill," she said, turning the page.

Her mother rolled her eyes behind Abuelita's back, making Alexis smile.

"Aha!" Alpha squealed with joy. "*Mira*, look

at that. They finally caught those rascals." She slapped her thigh with pleasure.

Alexis turned. "What are you talking about?"

Her grandmother beamed. "There was a drug bust last night out near Villa, and they caught all kinds of *narcos*," she cheered. Abuelita Alpha was obsessed with the lives of major drug dealers along the border. She talked about the infighting and who did what to whom like they were characters on television soap operas and not real-life criminals. But this news was different. Alexis had been near Villa last night.

"What happened?" Alexis asked, trying not to seem too interested.

"Aaah." Her *abuelita* winked. She raised her magnifying glass and read, "'US authorities uncovered a major drug-smuggling operation last night. Over twenty people were arrested at an illegal drag race, where they found over eight hundred pounds of marijuana.' *¡Híjole!*

That's a lot, no?" She looked at Alexis for confirmation.

"Arrested?" Alexis got up to peer at the article over her *abuelita*'s shoulder. There were pictures of trucks with the back doors wide open, revealing blocks of marijuana wrapped in plastic. She shivered.

"Scary, no?" her *abuelita* said, noting her reaction.

Alexis couldn't help but worry about Christian. She hadn't heard a word from him. He wasn't mixed up in drugs. Surely, the police wouldn't have been interested in him? Alexis knew he didn't do anything wrong. But would the authorities believe that? For as long as she could remember, the communities along the border had been riddled with violence and drug crime. People didn't like to talk about it, but it had seeped into all parts of their lives. "Let me see that," Alexis said, reaching for the paper.

"My paper," her *abuelita* snapped, holding the paper to her chest.

"Fine," Alexis sighed in frustration. "Read me some more, then."

Alpha smiled triumphantly and shook the paper out in front of her with great gusto. She raised her magnifying glass and read the rest of the article. There wasn't much more to tell. The authorities had been following a lead involving illegal drag races and drug trafficking for over two months. The roundup was considered a success and they hoped it would lead to more drug busts. Alexis sighed, feeling her heart flop. Well, at least there was no mention of Christian, she thought. That had to be a good sign. Then she thought of something.

"Abuelita, what happens to the guys who get caught? The ones mentioned in the article."

Her *abuelita* shot her a curious glance. "Do you know any of them?" she asked in a shocked tone.

"Of course I don't," Alexis said forcefully. She tried to smile. "I was just wondering, that's all."

Alpha studied her, squinting as if she could read Alexis's mind. She seemed to believe her and motioned for her to come closer. "I think they take them to a detention center, where they tie them up and try to get information out of them. They lock up some and toss the others to *el otro lado*."

Alexis jerked like she'd been slapped on the back with a ruler. "What do you mean they toss them to the other side?"

"The illegals. They deport those that don't have papers."

Christian, she thought, feeling her chest tighten. Alexis grabbed the back of her *abuelita*'s stool for support.

"*Mija*" — her *abuelita* studied her face — "are you all right? You look like you saw a ghost."

Alexis tried to breathe deeply. *I'm sure he got away. He probably lost his phone like I did, and hasn't gotten a chance to call another way.* "I'm fine," she said, trying to smile. "I think I just had too much hot chocolate and it gave me a head rush."

Her *abuelita* raised her index finger in a scolding manner. "You watch out with that chocolate, especially if Trini makes it." She leaned in and said in a hushed tone, "That stuff can make you loose. If you know what I mean."

As the hours turned into a full day, Alexis couldn't ignore her anxiety. There'd been no word from Christian. She thought about going to his house. But Mrs. Luna already didn't like her and probably wouldn't give her any information if she had some. Alexis chewed at what was left of her nails. She was going to lose her mind if she didn't get some news of Christian.

The door chimed and her cousin Santiago walked into her family's restaurant with a cheerful grin on his face. He stopped in front of the register with his arms akimbo and took a deep whiff. "What's good today?"

Then Santiago wandered to the back hallway

and Alexis followed him, assuming he was headed to the men's bathroom to wash his hands.

"Santiago, we have to talk," she said, following him inside and blocking the bathroom door behind her. She startled a customer who was drying his hands. Her cheeks reddened as she moved to let the guy leave.

"Whoa, Alexis, what's gotten into you? The men's bathroom is a sacred space for men only."

"It's Christian. I'm worried sick. His cell has been off and he hasn't returned any of my calls."

Suddenly, the door smacked Alexis on the bottom. "Hey," she snapped. "Occupied!"

"What are you two doing in there?" her big sister called through the door. "Let me in," she said, pushing her way inside. She glanced from Santiago back to Alexis. "You two are acting very strange. What are you up to?"

Alexis explained what had happened the other night, the drag races and the drug bust. Fabi's face darkened when she discovered where they'd been, but when Alexis got to the part about Christian, Fabi hugged her. Alexis relaxed into the embrace, thankful for her sister's understanding.

"We need to find him," Fabi said, putting her hands on her hips.

"Yes," Alexis cried, feeling her hope rise. Fabi always knew how to make things happen.

"But where do we start? If the cops picked him up, there are a bunch of jails and detention centers," Santiago said, sounding nervous.

Fabi pulled out her cell phone. "I'm going to call our cousin Bobby." Bobby Sanchez was a police officer. "He'll know what to do."

"Don't say nothing about me being at the races, all right?" Santiago said in a worried voice.

Officer Bobby Sanchez recommended that they check out the detention center in Hidalgo. Bobby didn't ask for any information, nor did Fabi volunteer any.

Santiago drove them to the detention center way out in the rural countryside. Alexis's heart sank as they approached the facility. A series of officelike gray buildings surrounded by a menacing barbed-wire fence loomed ahead of them. Alexis couldn't imagine Christian in this prison.

But Christian was there.

When Alexis, Fabi, and Santiago made it inside, they learned that the police had turned him over to some Immigration and Customs Enforcement agents. They were keeping him isolated while they questioned him about the drug bust. He was not allowed any visitors at the moment, except for his attorney.

For a minute, Alexis thought her heart had actually stopped. Her sister reached for her hand, just as Alexis burst into tears. Thankfully, her sister was there to do the talking. Fabi was good at keeping a cool head in tough situations. She managed to get the name of his attorney from the staff. As they headed out of the building, Alexis recognized a woman coming through security. She had a stern expression ironed on her face and caught Alexis's eye right away.

Alexis swallowed. She tried to give Christian's mom a comforting smile.

"Have you no shame," his mother said, walking up to Alexis. Her eyes were swollen from crying. "This is all your fault. I knew nothing good would come from his hanging with you!" she snapped. The group of people in the waiting area stopped to stare at the scene. "You bewitched my son. You put a spell on him. I know it, and now look what you've done." Mrs. Luna crumbled, falling into the arms of two security people who had approached her from behind.

Fresh tears pricked Alexis's eyes. This was her fault. She wanted to tell Mrs. Luna how much she cared for Christian and that she never meant for this to happen. But Alexis didn't dare. Mrs. Luna was like a wounded animal, ready to snap and dig her claws into the closest person.

"Let's go," Fabi said after a while. "There's nothing more we can do here." Alexis nodded and followed her sister and cousin.

At the door, she glanced back. Someone had brought Mrs. Luna a cup of water and another person was helping her to a chair. Alexis's heart felt heavy. She wished that she could have talked to Christian, or even just gotten a glimpse of him.

On the drive home, Alexis was haunted by Mrs. Luna's words. They cut deeply. Not only because she blamed herself for his arrest but also because of the love spell she had used to bring him into her life. The memory of her visit to the *botánica* came back clearly. She had wanted a love story of her own — but she hadn't wanted this.

chapter 11

A week later, Christian was still in custody. No one but his mother and lawyer were allowed to visit him. Alexis tried to stay positive. *They have to release him*, she told herself. *Christian was just at the wrong place at the wrong time.*

She tried to busy herself with rehearsals for the upcoming mariachi presentation. Even though the group hadn't raised all the money to purchase new mariachi suits, Castillo was still making them perform. However, all the performing they'd done in public to raise money had helped make their ragtag group a bit more confident. At the rate they were collecting money, they would be able to afford replacement uniforms very soon.

The night before their first competition, the ensemble piled into the yellow Dos Rios school bus. They were scheduled to begin at eight a.m. sharp, so they would have to drive all night to get there. Alexis took a seat near the back. Her cousin slid into the seat across from hers and put his legs up. The rest of the group filed in, taking seats, playing around, and shouting excitedly until AP Castillo yelled for everyone to be quiet. Alexis smiled at Nikki as she sat next to her with her backpack in one hand and a bag of home-cooked goodies in the other. The smell of brownies made Alexis perk up.

The bus roared to life. Alexis felt butterflies in her stomach. She put her nose to the cold window and watched as they drove out of town. She wished Christian were able to come see their first real performance. She knew he'd be proud. The bus was traveling northeast, past San Antonio. Alexis had never been so far from the Rio Grande Valley. She knew that when she became famous, she would have to get used to leaving the Valley. But that didn't soothe her aching heart.

The rocking motion of the bus mixed with the rural countryside soon lulled everyone to sleep. Alexis awoke in the middle of the night, when the bus suddenly stalled. She rubbed her eyes and yawned loudly.

"Are we here?" she asked, stretching and glancing out the window. It was dark outside and she couldn't make out anything.

Nikki opened a Tupperware bowl of Rice Krispies treats and passed them over. She shrugged at Alexis. "I don't know. Doesn't look like it," she said, squinting out the window.

Castillo was talking to the driver. Alexis leaned in to hear, but she couldn't understand a word over the chatter of waking students.

"Yo, Castillo, can I go take a leak?" Santiago asked, getting up.

Castillo waved him away like he was an annoying fly. The driver was shaking his head in irritation.

"I got to go bad," Santiago whined, dancing from one foot to the other.

"Fine," AP Castillo said, "but don't go too far. We have to get back on the road."

Then everyone wanted to go. Half the group followed Santiago out of the bus. Since there weren't any restrooms, students were using the lights of their cell phones to find a bush or tree to go behind. Alexis heard a tapping sound coming from outside her window. She turned, expecting to see Santiago's funny grin, but he wasn't there. Out of the corner of her eye, she thought she saw a flapping motion. But it was gone too quickly for her to be sure.

Alexis stood up. "I'm going to go see what's going on," she told Nikki, climbing over her and into the aisle.

As she approached, AP Castillo waved her

away. "Have a seat, Garza," he said in a commanding voice.

She noticed the driver scratching his head and trying to turn the ignition on. The bus didn't respond. It was dead. "What's wrong?" she asked.

The driver sighed and glanced from Alexis to AP Castillo. "We were driving and everything was fine, but then all of a sudden the engine stalled." He tried the knobs on the radio. Nada. "Everything is dead."

Suddenly, they heard screams outside. Students rushed through the narrow doorway, pushing and shoving their way through, blocking her view. Then she heard flapping. It was loud and strong like a steady heartbeat. The shape of a huge birdlike creature swooped in front of the bus. *What was that?* Alexis thought as she reflexively ducked.

"La Lechuza," the bus driver screamed. He covered his face in his hands and crouched

down behind the steering wheel. AP Castillo stared. His mouth hung wide open. The students cried out in fright, scampering over the seats to hide. Karina pulled out a rosary from under her shirt and started to pray in a shaky voice. Alexis stared at her in shock. She never knew Karina carried a rosary.

"We need a rope or a string," Justin said, coming down the aisle. The dark and deserted landscape was putting everyone on edge, but not him. Justin seemed calm and purposeful.

"How about a shoelace?" Pedro volunteered, holding up a white cord he'd removed from his sneakers.

Justin nodded and mumbled thanks as he made a series of knots on the string. Alexis was confused. How were the ties supposed to protect them from a scary witch-bird? Justin looked up at Alexis as if reading her mind. He blushed.

"My grandma always said whenever you saw *La Lechuza* you better tie a string with seven knots for protection."

"Lechuga?" Marisol asked, waking up slowly and mishearing "lettuce." How could she sleep through all the screaming? Alexis wondered. Marisol looked at her. "What's going on? Are we stopping for food?"

"Le-chu-za," Justin said slowly, "not *le-chu-ga*. You never heard about her?" Marisol shook her head. "She's a witch-bird that attacks people on deserted roads," he explained. "Some say *La Lechuza* is a bringer of death, and if you look her in the eyes she will take your soul."

"Where's Santiago?" Alexis asked when she realized he wasn't on the bus.

Then she saw him. The moonlight outlined Santiago's figure. He pulled back on something small in his hand as he shouted.

"Yeah, I ain't scared of you, owl! Take that." He shot a rock into the night.

The sound of the flapping wings was loud — louder than any bird Alexis had ever heard before. She watched as her cousin fearlessly confronted *La Lechuza* with a slingshot.

Suddenly, the bird swooped down, right at Santiago. He screamed as he reached for his head and dropped to the ground.

Alexis cried, "Santiago," as she slid past AP Castillo and out the bus door. Her heart pounded in her ears. The flapping sound came again. It was right above her head. Alexis hurried to shield her cousin from another attack. She heard the bird screech in her ear as it swooped past them.

"That bird is crazy," her cousin said, handing her a sharp rock.

Alexis looked around near her. Santiago had dropped his slingshot near the left bus tire when he was attacked. She grabbed it and aimed toward the sky. The flapping of the large wings interrupted the silence of the wilderness. In the glow from the moon, she was able to see the huge bird making a wide circle above the bus. Alexis aimed the rock at the owl's head.

The owl screeched as it dove at her. Her arms were shaking and sweat was dripping down her face. She watched as the crazed bird plunged straight for her. Its yellow eyes reminded her of the ones she'd seen from the restaurant patio. At the last possible moment, she released the shot.

A high-pitched shriek filled the air. The noise was so loud it almost sounded human. Then she heard the sound of something crash into the ground. Santiago squeezed her shoulder.

"Good shot, *prima*."

Suddenly, the bus woke up. The engine roared as the Johnny Cash song "Ring of Fire" came on the radio. Santiago and Alexis stared at each other.

"Get on the bus," AP Castillo hollered, hanging out the door.

They got back on the bus and drove away. Everyone stared as Santiago and Alexis made their way to their seats in the back.

No one wanted to say it, but seeing this strange owl the night before their very first competition was not a good sign.

When they finally arrived at the event the air was brisk and the sky overcast. The plaza was decorated festively. Tissue paper had been cut into elaborate decorations, and hung from tree to tree like shirts on a clothesline. There were balloons, a small stage, and food booths.

Little kids in mariachi outfits scurried past them.

"Whoa, check out the munchkins," Santiago laughed.

Alexis looked around and noticed that the only people dressed in mariachi uniforms were less than four feet tall. A realization came over her. She turned to AP Castillo. "Please tell me we aren't competing against children?"

Castillo was helping Pablo and Pedro unload the instruments from the back of the bus. He smiled at Alexis. "What difference does it make? A competition is a competition. I want you guys to get comfortable onstage."

Karina groaned as she climbed out of the bus. "Really, Castillo? That's so embarrassing.

I'm so glad no one I know is here. Hey, watch my harp, will ya," she scolded the twins as they set her instrument down heavily.

The group assembled under a tree to watch the performances while they waited for their turn. The group playing on the stage was really good. Their lead singer, a third grader with light brown hair, was wailing away to a Vicente Fernandez classic.

"Where are you guys from?" a small girl dressed in a gold *charro traje* and pigtails asked. Two girls in matching outfits stood behind her with their arms crossed in a defensive manner.

Alexis smiled at a cute girl with freckles. "We're from Dos Rios in the Rio Grande Valley."

"Dos Rios." The girl huffed and glanced at her friends. "That's where all the drug dealers are from, huh?" Her friends snickered.

Alexis stared in shock. This cute little girl was talking trash about her town. She glanced around for support. The twins saw the sur-prise on her face and came over to see what was going on.

"My daddy says that people from Dos Rios are all criminals and on welfare," the pigtailed girl continued. "You can't even afford real mariachi outfits." She glanced at her friends and giggled.

"Little girl," Pablo said in a low voice, "don't you know it's rude to talk to your elders like that?"

"Elders?" The girl laughed loudly, mak-ing an absurd face to her friends. "Our music teacher said that you guys must be real bad if you had to come all the way out here to com-pete against *kids*."

"Go away," Marisol cried, jumping out from behind Alexis. "Go away before I eat you."

Pigtail Girl jumped back and ran away with her two friends. As she ran she yelled, "I bet they can't even stay in tune" to her friends and laughed.

"I hate kids," Marisol said as she sat back down on the grass.

Alexis looked from her to the twins and at the rest of the group. "Did you hear what she said about us? That was so rude."

Karina shrugged. "It's not like I'm surprised. Dos Rios has a bad reputation, you know. People are always judging us. They look at Pablo's and Pedro's shaved heads and baggy clothes and they see thugs. They look at me and probably think I'm trashy."

"They think I'm a freak." Marisol grinned.

"Thief," said Santiago.

"Illegal," added Nikki.

"Fat," said Justin.

Alexis's eyes grew wide at their words. She couldn't believe what she was hearing. What were her friends talking about?

"A has-been jock," AP Castillo said, joining the conversation. "But so what?" He stood up and looked every one of them in the eye. "People are always going to try to tell you who

[173]

you are. It's the way the world is." He clapped his thick hands together, making Alexis jump. "So what? Are we going to cry about it?"

"Hell no," Santiago swore.

AP Castillo couldn't help a small smile. "That's right. Maybe we come from a poor community and maybe we have our share of crime — but we're more than that."

Alexis felt something flutter in her chest. She didn't know what it was, but it was a warming sensation spreading all over her body.

AP Castillo gestured for the group to come closer. "We are Dos Rios," he said. "Most people here probably haven't heard of Dos Rios. Or they believe what they see on TV about border towns. But we can prove them wrong. We can show them all that we're much more than their stereotypes. When you get on that stage, you stand with your heads held high. Don't worry if you miss a note or come in at the wrong time — just keep playing. Whatever happens today, whether we win or lose, you're all winners in my book." He paused to study their reaction. "Look how far you've all come. Karina —" She looked up in surprise. "You haven't had one fight since you started mariachi. Pablo, Pedro, I've never seen the walls so empty of graffiti. Marisol —" She jumped. "Your counselor said you haven't cut class once this month. And Santiago . . ."

"Yes, MR. ASSISTANT . . ." Santiago smiled, waiting for his compliment.

"I don't have to chase you anymore."

"That's right and . . ."

"And . . . what?"

"And I'm your new favorite accordion player," Santiago suggested, sliding the accordion over his shoulder and playing a quick melody. He winked. Castillo began to chuckle.

Alexis laughed with him. "He's right," she said, finding her voice.

"We've been through a lot these past few weeks," Castillo continued. "Look at us. We're all still here. The Dos Rios mariachi group is not made up of quitters. Maybe we don't have fancy outfits and we're still learning how to play, but we have the most important thing —"

"We have passion," Alexis and Justin said at the same time. Their eyes locked and they smiled.

Castillo nodded with a gleam in his eyes. "When you're up there playing our music, own it. Mariachi music is the music of the working classes. The people. No one can take the music away from us."

When it was their time to perform, Alexis took the mic and smiled at the audience. The crowd looked tired. She focused on the trees lining the park to calm her nerves. Then she turned to glance at the members of the maria-chi ensemble. Their smiles gave her all the strength she needed to sing. Alexis smiled as the guitars started to strum their chords, followed by the horns, and finally her cousin began to jam on his accordion behind her.

Alexis took a deep breath and opened her mouth to sing.

The Dos Rios mariachi group played their hearts out to a standing ovation. Because of their competitors' ages, and the friendly nature of the competition, there weren't any prizes awarded, but that didn't seem to bother the members much. They had tried their best, and everyone in the audience had felt their enthusiasm. The ride back was festive, with lots of impromptu singing of mariachi songs like "Por un Amor," "La Malagueña," and "La Media Vuelta." They sang along to "Bidi Bidi Bom Bom," "No Tengo Dinero," and other Selena and Kumbia Kings classics the bus driver had on his CD player. It was late when they finally got back home to Dos Rios.

Alexis's heart swelled when she saw the "Dos Rios" welcome sign, proclaiming it to be "the home of the big enchilada, population 6,956." She couldn't help but be proud to represent Dos Rios. Looking at the faces of her friends on the bus, she hoped they would stay committed to showing people how great a group of high school students from a small town could be.

Suddenly, her new phone rang, playing a short mariachi melody. She didn't recognize the number, but she went ahead and picked up.

"Alexis, it's me, Christian. How are you?"

Alexis screamed, "Oh, Christian! I'm so happy to finally hear from you. I've been so worried, and they wouldn't let me in to visit you. How are you? Listen, we're actually driving back from our first mariachi performance. Can you believe it? Us. Performing onstage. It was amazing. We completely won the audience's hearts." Alexis could feel herself babbling, but she couldn't stop. It was so good to finally hear his voice. "Are you out?"

"Um, sort of." Christian paused. "I knew you guys could do it, that's great," he continued.

"Where are you? Come to the restaurant. We're going to have a little party — nothing big, just the families and friends. I can't wait to see you. I've been so worried. But today has been the best day, and now with you free everything is perfect."

"I would love to, but . . ."

Alexis covered her left ear with her hand. She could barely hear him over the noise on the bus. They were approaching the school and she could see that there was a crowd of family members waiting in the parking lot. Alexis pressed the phone to her ear to better hear Christian.

"What is it?" Alexis asked.

"Well, they cleared me of any drug-related charges."

"That's great. I knew they would."

"But . . ."

"But what?" Alexis asked. Why was he acting like this? It was making her stomach squirm.

"They're . . . they're deporting me back to Mexico."

"What?" Alexis, confused, felt her heart drop. "I don't . . ."

"I leave this afternoon."

"I don't understand." Alexis fell back into her seat. She felt like she'd been punched in the stomach. His words became jumbled. It didn't make sense. Deported? Her perfect day burst into a hundred billion pieces. The bus had stopped. Her bandmates streamed off into the parking lot, but Alexis was unable to move.

"Christian, I'm so sorry." Her voice cracked. "This is all my fault. I will never forgive myself for taking you to the races. I never should have left you — I should have made Santiago stay and look for you —"

"It's not your fault." Christian sounded tired. "The police never would have bothered with me if I hadn't been hanging around with the Salinas brothers." Alexis could hear the bitterness in his voice. She wished she could give him a hug. "Listen, I have to go, but I wanted to call and let you know that I'm okay."

Alexis wiped away the tears that were rolling down her cheeks. "This is horrible. What about your scholarship? All your dreams? What about us?"

Christian was quiet. It put Alexis on edge. She heard voices cheering loudly from outside the bus. But Alexis felt like she was miles away.

"Is this it?" she asked in a quiet voice.

"I don't know what to tell you. This is as much a shock to me as it is to you. I have no idea where I'll live, how I'll eat, and no idea of my future."

"I can help you," Alexis said, feeling pressure on her heart as if someone were pressing a weight to her chest. "Please let me. I can get you a better lawyer. We'll find a way to get you back."

He was silent again. "What you need to do is concentrate on whipping that mariachi group into shape. I'm not going to go easy on you guys at next year's regional competition just because I have a crush on your group's lead singer," he joked.

Alexis couldn't help but laugh. "We'll practice. I promise." Alexis felt tears welling up in her eyes again. "I miss you."

"I miss you, too. But we'll see each other again." He paused and for a second Alexis wondered if the call had been dropped. "Do you remember those lyrics you sang so beautifully to me on my driveway?"

Alexis felt herself blush. Of course she remembered. She had practiced the song over a hundred times in the mirror. Alexis started to softly sing "Me Gustas Mucho" to Christian.

As she sang, the words held new meaning to her. When she had first sung the song she was a hopeful girl trying to attract the eye of a cute boy. Now when she sang about not letting anyone or anything keep him from her she thought about the US border patrol and the Rio Grande River that physically kept them apart.

When she finished, Christian gave a heart-felt laugh. "Well, then I guess you'll keep chasing after me, huh?"

"I guess."

"And you promise not to let anyone or any border keep you from chasing me?"

"Yes." She shrugged. "Why not? Saving *charros* just so happens to be a hobby of mine."

He laughed again. "Well then, I'll have to keep you close, very close."

They said good-bye. Alexis took a deep breath and stared at the "call ended" screen. Alexis looked up at the sound of someone calling her name. Santiago stood at the front of the bus motioning for her to come outside. She took a deep breath to steady her nerves and got up. At the door, she noticed her grandma Trini and Abuelita Alpha holding signs with her name up over their heads. Alexis glanced around the group, at all the families that had gathered to celebrate the return of the Dos

Rios mariachi team. There was a newfound gleam in her bandmates' eyes. She noticed a quiet confidence in the way the twins shared the highlights of the trip with their mother, real excitement in Karina's voice as she made her family pose for pictures with her harp, and genuine friendship in the way Nikki introduced Marisol to her family. Everywhere she turned, the Dos Rios mariachi ensemble glowed with pride, power, and team spirit. They had *finally* felt the music.

acknowledgments

Many thanks to all the fabulous people who continue to support the Border Town series. Specifically, I'd like to thank Amanda Maciel, Anna Bloom, the entire Scholastic team, and my super agent Stefanie Von Borstel. I also want to thank Dolores Josefina Ibarra Reyes and her family at San Jalisco restaurant for sharing their stories and food with me. Thank you to Jose Lopez for rescuing my computer not once, but several times. *Muchísimas gracias* to Rosario, Michael Arreola-Pro, and Nishat Kurwa for providing me with a great space to

write. To Nikki Garza, Lizby Munoz, Roxy Gonzalez, Tabby Sue Brocha, Maria Elena Ingram, Juan *y* Maria Elena Ovalle, Cynthia Perales *y sus comadres*, and Juan Salazar and his AVID class at Brown Middle School, thanks for providing me with great stories, reading drafts, and answering all my crazy questions. To the Weslaco High mariachi group and to mariachi teachers and students everywhere, thanks for keeping the *cultura* alive. And lastly to my family, *gracias por aguantarme* during these last few crazy months — love you all!